NO CLEARANCE TO TERRA

Trouble came from three directions at once, lambent green fire circling the tapering bases of slender shapes, vessels like sharks, long, narrow, vicious, arrowing in for the kill.

They fell away as Kennedy fed power to the drive, as he sent the *Mordain* nearer the sun, to a point above the third planet, the world which was Earth.

They fell toward the mottled green, brown and blue ball traced with fleecy white clouds, blotched with menacing shapes. Orbiting forts of peculiar construction, treble cones joined at the bases to form three-pointed stars. Fire blasted from one, a thick finger of green flame, and the *Mordain* jerked to the impact of violent energies . . .

What sort of a
welco

Earth
Enslaved

A "CAP KENNEDY" NOVEL

by Gregory Kern

DAW BOOKS, INC.

DONALD A. WOLLHEIM, PUBLISHER

1301 Avenue of the Americas
New York, N. Y.   10019

FIRST PRINTING, JUNE, 1974

1 2 3 4 5 6 7 8 9

PRINTED IN U.S.A.

CHAPTER ONE

From his seat at the controls Elg Rowan could see the screens, ranked dials, the reflection of his own face in a polished strip of metal. A hard face, no longer young, seamed and stamped with the vicissitudes of time. He scowled at it, not liking what he saw, wondering if it had turned into the visage of a fool.

The thought bothered him and he lifted his eyes, staring at the vista of space limned with crystal clarity on the screens. Stars shining with remote hostility, the pale fuzz of distant nebulas, ebon splotches of interstellar dust which hid the luminescence beyond. He looked with casual indifference at the familiar scene before adjusting the magnification to scan an area of space close to hand.

Nothing.

Nothing on the screens, nothing on the instruments, and no sign of activity from the expensive Larvik-Shaw spatial disturbance detector which his new partners had insisted that he install. The thought of them deepened his scowl. Forty years of tough living, risking his neck a thousand times, and now doing it again on the ghost of a promise. If this trip proved a bust he was finished, back to where he had started as a dewy-eyed boy in his teens with starlight in his eyes and romance in his soul.

The starlight had faded and the romance had died, but the itch remained. The hope that, this time, he would make it. The big strike, the bonanza, the jackpot which would make him rich and let him coast on a tide of luxury. It had happened, Eng Kyle had done it, Heeb Moreton, Ole Elverum—the names rolled in his mind like the beat of drums. A handful among thousands, but they had proved it was possible. All a man needed was guts and luck. Forty years had proved he had the guts and now, surely, it was time for a little luck.

Rising, he crossed to the Larvik-Shaw. The screen incorporated into the apparatus showed a thin tracery of delicate lines as highly sensitive detectors reached into space to locate any disturbance. An electromagnetic storm would cause the instrument to respond. A nearby mass, a gravitational node, any alteration in the normal continuum—but as yet there had been nothing.

Irritably he slammed the heel of his palm against the casing.

"Steady on, Pop, that thing cost money."

Neil Quimper was half Rowan's age and looked a third. Neatly combed hair rested above a smoothly round face, the lips quirked in a perpetual smile, the eyes blue and bright with intelligence. He stepped into the control room and glanced at the screen, the instruments.

"Nothing yet?"

"No." Rowan glared his irritation. "I'm beginning to doubt if there ever will be. Three weeks now we've been looking and still no sign. I thought you had this all figured out."

Quimper shrugged, his voice casual. "Not me, Pop. José Oveido. I just helped to provide the cash, remember?"

He was a spoiled scion of a wealthy family taking a look around the system before settling down to a nice, snug desk job. Yet his aid had been essential. Money for fuel, supplies, the expensive detector, and to pay the creditors who were holding the ship. His money, Rowan's vessel, and Oveido's knowledge.

His voice was calm as he joined the others.

"No luck as yet, my friend? Well, it is to be expected. We are looking for a mote of dust in an ocean of emptiness. And yet my calculations show that it must be close."

Rowan said bitterly, "Unless you figured wrong."

"Not I, my friend." Oveido, middle-aged, rumpled as if he had slept in his clothes, shrugged as he spread his hands in an age-old gesture. "If anything is to be blamed it is the computer at Madrid. My calculations were most precise and were based on starcharts spread over a hundred years. Zafra exists. You know why I called it that? After my wife, may her soul rest in peace. She, too, was elusive and, she too, held great treasure. Treasure, my friend, which we shall find."

That promise had lured him from the Belt to a point a full astronomical unit outside the orbit of Pluto and another above the plane of the ecliptic. Rowan moved, impatient with himself and the others, knowing again the searing bitterness of failure.

"A dream," he said. "I should have known better."

"No dream," said Oveido quickly. "A careful deduction based on scientific fact. As you know, my friend. As I explained to you so very many times."

Quimper and Oveido had met in the Hive at Ceres where they had drifted, an ill-matched pair, looking for someone like Rowan. And yet Rowan had to be fair. He had been willing to be convinced, eager to clear his ship and again be on the search. And their words had made sense.

A fragment of a destroyed world as the asteroids were, this one was on an eccentric path which carried it far beyond the Solar System into the darkest regions of space beyond Pluto. A fragment of something which could have wandered from a distant galaxy, perhaps, to be caught by the gravitational pull of the sun and flung, like a comet, into a tremendously elongated elliptical orbit.

Soon it would be detected by the watchful eyes of Terran Control, and then taken and examined by the ships of MALACA 1 which guarded the system. But if Rowan and his partners could reach it first, their claim would be recognized and it and the treasure it might contain would be theirs beyond question.

Gems, perhaps, minerals, rare metals, even artifacts

of some ancient race. The discovery alone would be of
value. Fame and fortune at last!

"You see, Pop," said Quimper, "the last time it entered our system was way back before space travel was
what it is now. Thanks to José here we've got a chance
to get in first. He's plotted the orbit as best he could,
now the rest is up to us. It's out there, somewhere." He
gestured at the screen. "All we have to do is find it."

"Sure," said Rowan savagely. "But how?"

"Don't ask me, Pop, that's in your department."
Quimper crossed to the Larvik-Shaw. "But this should
make it easy."

If it was there to be found. If Oveido had calculated
correctly. If nothing had happened to the fragment on
its long, long journey around the sun.

Rowan glared at the screen, seeing only the familiar
tracery of delicate lines, resisting the impulse to hit it
again, to send the ship into random flight. A search had
to follow a pattern. He had taken the figures Oveido
had provided and formed a wide-flung area of investigation. They were following it now as they had done
for the past three weeks. In a couple of days it would
be completed, and if they hadn't found anything, the
trip would have been a wasted effort.

On the screen the lines flickered a trifle.

"Pop!" Quimper had noticed. "Is that—"

"Shut up!" Rowan concentrated on the screen. Again
came the flicker and then, abruptly, the lines twisted,
converging to form a pattern like a spider's web, thin at
the edges and thick at the center. They dissolved as he
adjusted a control, returned firmer than before.

His voice rose in a shout of triumph.

"That's it! It has to be! By God, we've found it!"

It was small, a scrap of rugged stone which barely reflected the light, seeming to drink the radiance, to absorb it as if it were a sponge. Rowan snapped off the
beams as the ship settled, frowning as he read the instruments.

"It's dense," he commented. "Which means the rock

must have a high mineral content. At a guess I'd say it was a nickel-iron combination. Well, we'll soon find out."

Suited, he led the others from the air-lock, gekko-boots holding them firm to the scrap of debris. Without wasted effort, following a pattern he had learned years before, Rowan set up a spectroscope, and lifting his Dione from its holster, fired a lambent shaft of flame at the rocks before the scanner.

"No good," he said as he read the dials. "This stuff must be close to absolute zero. We'll have to fire together. At the same point, three charges each, now!"

Nine blasts of raw energy lashed at the rock, minute portions of unstable isotopes yielding their energy in the firing chambers, the blasts focused and controlled by permanent magnets in the finned barrels of the Diones. Heat turned the rock to molten slag, sent little runnels of metal oozing from the point of impact, a thin plume of vapor rising to dissipate in the void.

"That's better." Over the radio Rowan's voice held satisfaction. "High metallic content as I suspected. Iron, nickel, some copper, and traces of platinum and gold. Plenty of carbon too. It's a rough assay, but one thing's for sure. We're going to show a profit if nothing else."

"Let's look it over." Oveido was shrill with excitement. "Do you realize just what this is? The proof of my investigations. A fragment of planetary debris on which no man has ever trod before this moment. I suspected that it might exist and now we have found it. Those who laughed at me for being a dreamer will have cause to smile on the other side of their mouths. Zafra, our own world to do with as we please. We must file our claim immediately."

Quimper said, in a strange tone, "Here! Look at this!"

He was standing close to where the shafts of flame from the Diones had gouged a patch from the rock. As the others moved toward him he drew his gun and fired, flame spurting up from the sides of a narrow hole, limning his suited figure with crimson light.

"What is it?" Oveido shoved himself forward, moving clumsily in his suit, the gekko-boots clinging to the rock.

"Metal." Quimper pointed, his helmet-beam illuminating the area at his feet. "Solid metal beneath the stone. See?"

Rowan knelt, probing with the barrel of his Dione, cursing at the inadequacy of the tool. A shard of rock fell away to vanish into space beneath the thrust of an impatient hand. More followed to reveal a smooth surface of metal which showed dull and gray in the beams of their lights.

"What the hell is it?" whispered Quimper. "It's artificial, that's obvious, but what can it be for?"

"And who built it?" Oveido was solemn. "Do you realize just how old this must be?"

Rowan straightened, feeling himself expand with the shock of accomplishment. For a moment he suffered a sudden vertigo so that the stars seemed to whirl and explode in bright gouts of flame as if they were elements in a fireworks display.

The jackpot!

Against the value of the artifact the metallic content of the rock was as nothing. No matter what was contained under the smooth surface it would be of incredible value to scientists if no one else. The bonanza!

After forty years of looking he had found it.

He said unsteadily, "We need explosives, tools, cutting equipment. This area must be cleared."

"Couldn't we let others do that?" Quimper was uncertain. "I mean—"

"We found it," Oveido interrupted fiercely. "We have the right."

"It was my money—"

"And my calculations! Without me you would have found nothing. I say we look!"

Rowan felt the butt of the Dione beneath his hand.

He could lift it and fire. Two shots and it would be over, the discovery his to enjoy alone.

And then, firmly, he released his hold on the weapon.

"Listen," he said harshly. "You've begun to argue and I know where that can lead. Forty years in space has taught me one thing. Either you rely on your partners or you're dead. Which is it to be?"

His helmet beam caught Quimper's face as the man turned toward him.

"Pop?"

"Your money, maybe," snapped Rowan. "José's brains and my ship. Neither of us could have done it alone. Now we'll have a vote. Either we let things go as they are or we take a look at what's to be found. Majority rules. I'm for taking a look. Oveido?"

"I'm with you."

"I'm against."

"Two to one, Quimper. You lose. Now let's get at it."

Four decades as a prospector had given Rowan skill. He knew just where to drill, how powerful the charges should be, just where to move the ship to a place of safety. Within hours they had cleared a wide area of rock to expose the metal surface. After the final blast something new was revealed, a circular plate which had to be a means of entry to whatever lay beneath.

"Careful." Tired as they all were Quimper could have thought for the future. "We don't want to damage anything. That could be an airtight seal."

"So what?" Rowan stooped over the fastenings with a lastorch, the beam cutting into metal as, stubbornly, it yielded to the intense heat.

"If it is, and if air is still inside there, you could get hurt by the blast."

Rowan lifted the torch and blinked sweat from his eyes. He was sagging with fatigue and should rest, but excitement made sleep an impossibility.

"I'll drill a small hole," he decided. "If there is air or gas below we can seal it. Get me something to make a test; a heap of fine dust will do it."

Again he lowered the torch, metal flowing, vaporizing as the beam dug deeper. Abruptly it ceased to flare, the hole widening, the dust thrown over it drifting, untouched by any rising current.

"No air." Rowan returned his attention to the fastenings. "Now let's get this damn thing open. Get some lights and fresh tanks from the ship, Quimper. Oveido, you get a couple of levers and stand ready to slip them into the opening I'll make at the rim. Once these clamps are gone we should be able to heave it open."

It wasn't as easy as that. For minutes they strained at the levers, and then, losing patience, Rowan burned a jagged opening through the center of the plate.

In the glow of a suspended light they looked inside.

"Machines," Quimper said wonderingly. "Or maybe the whole thing is a machine. Look at those connections, those bars. And could that be a power source?"

Oveido said tersely, "Let's get inside."

The thing was vast, a tremendous circular compartment which reached into the distance so that the beams of their lights seemed to dwindle and be lost in a host of stark shadows, lightless areas cast by looming constructions of unguessed purpose.

On all sides rested enigmatic columns of milky substance, their surfaces graduated with regularly spaced lines. Other apparatus, equally enigmatic, hung on supports reaching from equidistant points of the compartment so that they ran directly along the central axis. And, like the compartment itself, they were huge.

"I feel like an ant." Rowan's voice held an undertone of awe. "Like a damned ant walking in a powerhouse. What could all this be for?"

"How can we tell?" Oveido was solemn. "Giants could have built it, or pygmies. Things that have no relationship with human life as we know it. Remember how incredibly old it must be. Long before life had left the oceans the planet of which this must have been a part had broken and cast remnants of itself into the void." His helmet beam flashed over the central apparatus, the milky columns, the thick bars of gleaming metal. "Old," he whispered again. "So very old."

Quimper moved down the compartment, his gekko-boots leaving a faint trail in the thin patina of dust. He was a little awkward, unused to the suction of the boots, lifting each leg high at the knee. He paused at one of the thick bars.

"Gold," he said quietly. "It has to be. Either gold or some unknown alloy. Any other metal would have dulled over the course of time." He moved on, lost in speculation, his voice a soft mutter from the radio. "Units in series it seems like . . . a cascade effect if those machines are what I think they must be . . . heavy-duty conduits . . . focal point for directed energy . . . why?"

None of them could answer that question.

Instinctively Rowan checked his meters, a reflex action born of long training. The fresh tanks of air Quimper had brought from the vessel would last a while yet and he was eager to learn all he could. Help would have to be summoned now, that was certain; this was a job for trained scientists and skilled technicians, but there could be other things than the enigmatic apparatus. Some smaller artifacts might be found and hidden away for later, private sale.

He would never get a chance like this again.

As Oveido moved after the other man Rowan stepped to one side, hurrying a little as he headed toward the far end of the compartment. The suspended units ended to be replaced by a series of rods set in a circle and aimed at a common point. Before it, set on spidery supports, a fragment of black metal rested in direct line with the snout of the final unit and the open space between the rods. Surrounding it in a series of reflective facets sheets of a crystalline substance caught the beam of his light and shimmered in a sudden burst of effulgent splendor.

"What's that?" Quimper lunged forward, forgetting the low, almost nonexistent gravity and rising sharply upward as his gekko-boots lost their hold. He spun, collided with the supports of the black metal, grunted as a stanchion gouged into his side.

"Steady!" Rowan reached up and pulled him down. "You hurt?"

"No." Quimper was shaken. "Bruised a little, but that's all."

"You sure?" Rowan had caught the note of pain in the transmitted voice. "You could have cracked a rib. Try a deep breath." He frowned at the sudden, sharp inhalation. "Get back to the ship," he ordered. "Take it slow and easy. We'll follow."

"No! I want to see what this is all about." Quimper was stubborn. "That fragment of black metal looks like it could be a target of some kind. Or, no, perhaps . . ." His voice faded as he caught a support and lifted himself higher. "It seems as if once it was much larger than it is now. A cube which fitted the supporting clamps. It must have decayed by natural disintegration over the years. It—" He broke off, his voice heavy with pain.

"You are hurt, my friend." Oveido joined him, their suited figures clinging to the supports. "Let me help you down. It would be best to do as Rowan suggests. Return to the ship and wait for us. We will not be long."

"I just want to see—" Quimper reached out and tugged at a delicate strand of metal. "See? As I thought. This rod should have remained in contact with the support. As the metal decayed and grew smaller it would have followed this path here . . . and touched there . . . and—"

He cried out, his breath rasping, liquid.

"Back!" Rowan was firm. "Get back to the ship at once. That's an order and you'll obey it unless you're a fool. From the sound of it you've ripped a lung and you'll drown in your own blood unless you take care. Oveido, help him."

"And you?"

"I'll be along." Rowan watched as they moved slowly down the compartment toward the opening, more pleased than annoyed at the turn of events. Now he would be free of watchful eyes. He added, "You might as well record our claim while you're at it."

Delay could be dangerous, others might have followed them and be waiting to take over. Such things had happened before. Alone he quested the forward area, tugging at a bar of metal, pausing as he caught the splinter of fire from a column crusted with gems.

It reared from the floor, apparently unconnected with any of the other apparatus, a rod three feet in height by five inches thick. He tugged at it and felt a firm resistance. Impatiently he snatched at his Dione.

Time was running out. His air was getting low and the others would be waiting. Now, if ever, was his chance to make a private haul.

Crimson fire bathed the foot of the column as he triggered the release. Metal softened, flowed beneath the impact of the searing heat of the shafts of energy, and reflected light shimmered from the suspended units, the circle of rods, the milky columns to either side.

Light which did not die.

Rowan paused as he tugged at the gem-encrusted lever, eyes wide behind his faceplate as he stared at the enigmatic devices. The columns were now glowing with a host of lambent colors, red, green, orange, purple, vivid blue, the graduations clear against the inner luminescence. As he watched a nimbus of eerie light shone over the suspended units, flaring with a cold emerald, rippling as if from inner turmoil.

Abruptly the circle of rods pulsed with a nacreous light.

Rowan released his hold on the gemmed column and ran. He thrust himself forward, gekko-boots sucking at the smooth floor, slowing his progress so that he seemed to be in a nightmare in which he ran from some terrible danger but slowed as he ran so that it came closer, closer.

He ignored the voice from his radio.

"Rowan! What's WRONG? What's happened, man?"

Oveido caught the sounds of his labored breathing, his panic. "Damn it, man, answer!"

Rowan fell, landing awkwardly, one ankle twisting, helmet ringing to the impact of metal. He turned, clamping one foot to the floor, rising, eyes widening as he stared back at the far end of the compartment.

Now the rods were alive with shimmering radiance, the suspended units pulsing with ever-increasing frequency, milky light merging with emerald, motes of dust rising, spinning, caught in electronic energies which gave them a horrible semblance of life. And in the open space between the circle of rods, something was happening.

Rowan screamed.

He turned and ran as if wading through mud, falling, rising to lunge onward, rising to hit against the glowing columns, arms and legs wildly moving as he fought to regain traction, falling again for one last time to touch a glowing bar of bright metal, to vanish in a sudden puff of vapor, a pinch of drifting ash.

CHAPTER TWO

In the workshop of the *Mordain* a giant sat building a web. He sat, huge on the stool, eyes clamped to a magnifier, broad, thick-fingered hands amazingly deft as he manipulated instruments, soldering points as fine as wire, tweezers which looked like gossamer to the naked eye. Anyone unfamiliar with Penza Saratov would have thought him incapable of this occupation.

It would have been a natural reaction. Almost as wide as he was tall, the shaven ball of his head mounted on a thick neck which sloped to massive shoulders, he was a living machine of flesh, bone, and muscle. Born and reared on a world with three times the gravity of Earth he was reminiscent of a troglodyte of ancient mythology. Dressed in his usual loose robes he looked like a man grown obscenely fat, a casual assumption he had often used to advantage. Now, as he made the final connection, he leaned back and expelled his breath with a sigh.

It was a contented sound. The engines of the *Mordain* hummed with a quiet efficiency, the triple coils matched to seven nines of similarity, one place more than that aimed for by the fleet technicians, two more than the absolute minimum. One day he would manage to tune them even closer, to get as near as possible to absolute perfection.

Picking up the device on which he had labored he left the workshop and entered the laboratory where Kennedy sat with Luden, a sheaf of papers littering the desk between them.

"Ah, Penza." Luden looked up as the giant entered. "Finished?"

"I've completed the pilot model, Jarl. I had to adapt one of the components but it will work as specified. At least I hope so. The trouble with miniaturized communicators is that they tend to build up residual charges and so gain an inbuilt source of white noise. And on highly civilized worlds there is enough interference anyway." He held out the construct. "Here, try it."

It was as beautiful as a jewel. Wafer-thin, set on a wide band of gleaming metal cut with a prismatic pattern that caught and reflected the light in rainbow shimmers, it seemed to float on the palm of his hand. A raised portion held a tiny screen, sensitive patches serving as controls.

Luden pursed his lips as he examined it.

"My congratulations, Penza. You have an unexpected streak of artistry. Cap?"

Kennedy took it in turn, turning it, feeling the weight and balance.

"Efficiency?"

"Close range, Cap, it can't be anything else." The giant shrugged. "We're up against certain barriers. The power source for one, the input-output ratio for another. And then there is the problem of noise. Make it sensitive enough to receive a faint signal and you automatically pick up everything else on the same band. Install filters and you increase bulk—but you know the problem. A simple voice communicator now, that's simple. I could build one in a ring, but when you want vision, color, and three-dimensional portrayal, well, it isn't easy."

"Difficulties, Penza, are there to be overcome."

"Try telling that to a man trying to get a quart in a pint pot, Jarl," said Saratov dryly. "Maybe he'll give you an answer."

Luden sniffed. Against the giant he looked a wisp, thin, frail, his stringy body dressed in shirt and pants edged with glowing colors, more color at his waist, the flare of his collar. A mass of grayish hair rose from a high forehead. His lips were thin, downturned as if he had tasted something not to his liking. His eyes, vividly blue, were alight with intelligence.

Smiling, Kennedy said, "You've done well, Penza. Now let's see if you are as good at making coffee. But, please, this time, could we have it without all your secret additions?"

Offended, the giant said, "If you don't like my coffee you can always drink the rubbish Veem turns out."

"No," said Luden quickly. "If anything he is worse than you are. Just use your skill on the coffeepot and we'll all be happy."

As Saratov grunted and moved toward the galley he picked up the construct and slipped it on his wrist. The band, made for a normal arm, was too loose. Slipping it off, Luden laid it down and looked thoughtfully at it.

"A problem, Cap, but one which could be overcome. In any case it does tend to bear out the theory of a highly technological race having contacted Earth in early history. Legends are full of magical bracelets and devices with which to communicate with the gods. I think it no accident that much primitive jewelry seems to bear a relationship with modern artifacts. Why, for example, should bracelets bear shaped sections of stone? For decoration, perhaps, or could it be an attempt to simulate something barely remembered, a pattern handed down from generation to generation? We know for a fact that the Zheltyana Seal has been so used, a pattern remembered and used as a good luck symbol by a wide variety of cultures who have no knowledge of the Zheltyana at all."

"It could be coincidence, Jarl."

"Perhaps," admitted Luden. "In a few cases the possibility of coincidence must be recognized, but we have accumulated enough evidence to be positive that the Zheltyana must have contacted if not occupied almost every world in the galaxy. The similarity of cultural habits such as the use of the Ancient Sign is too widespread to admit of doubt. As are the legends. If we are able to construct a device like this miniature sight-and-sound transceiver, then why shouldn't they have been common once?"

Trade goods, perhaps, or toys to amuse the primitive races, monitoring instruments even so that various experiments in cultural relationships could be conducted. There was no way of telling.

Kennedy leaned back, his eyes misted with thought as he looked at the books and records bearing on the great mystery of the Zheltyana. Aeons ago a race with tremendous scientific achievement had flowered to spread over the known worlds of the galaxy to suddenly vanish without trace leaving only fragments of their presence behind. Where had they come from and where had they gone? And, more important, what had happened to their incredible technology?

Questions which, one day, he hoped to answer.

The sound of the communicator broke his reverie.

Elias Weyburn, Director of Terran Control, looked like a brooding eagle. His face was seamed, the jowls sagging, the eyes hooded and pouched. His nose was a beak that thrust over his mouth and his shoulders were rounded. He said without preamble, "Cap, there's trouble."

"Where?"

"Right here," said Weyburn grimly. "Right smack in our own backyard."

"Such as?"

"I'm not sure yet, but it smells." One finger lifted to unconsciously rub the prominent nose. "It smells and it's close. Too damn close for comfort."

"On Earth?"

"Not yet, thank God."

Kennedy frowned. It was not like Weyburn to be evasive and it was a sure measure of his concern that he seemed reluctant to give details. And the concern was justified. Weyburn walked a perpetual tight-rope like an acrobatic juggler keeping balls high in the air while others tried to snare his feet.

Kennedy was one of those who helped him to keep his balance.

He said, "Tell me about it."

"I'd rather you saw it first. Get here as fast as you can." Weyburn gave the coordinates. "And, Cap . . ."

"Yes?"

"Hurry!"

The screen died, too soon, too abruptly, as if Weyburn was afraid that someone, somewhere, might be listening to the exchange—an impossibility with the special equipment used. Kennedy turned, thoughtful, remembering the added lines of strain on the heavy features, the expression in the hooded eyes.

There had been fear there and something else. A touch of dread, of panic, as if the Director had been faced with an impossible situation, and, for once, had found himself unable to handle it.

A direct threat to Earth?

It was possible, the given coordinates were close; whatever it was would be within the system, and Kennedy had sensed the fear behind the summons.

At first glance the control room was empty, then something blurred in the chair and took the shape of a man. Chemile was tall and thin, with an upsweep of hair above a sloping brow, pointed and convoluted ears which hugged his skull, and eyes like tiny gems in the smooth ovoid of his face. He was the product of an ancient race on a harsh world and he had a peculiar ability. His skin, scaled with minute flecks of photosensitive tissue, could adopt the coloration of any background against which he stood. A man-sized chameleon with an infinitely superior protective mechanism, consciously controlled and amazingly adaptable.

"Cap?"

"Give me the chair, Veem." Kennedy sat at the controls and fed the coordinates into the computer. Power flowed from the engines as he sent the vessel on its new direction, a mounting thrust which destroyed time and distance.

Watching, Chemile said, "Trouble, Cap?"

"I'm not sure." As a member of the team Chemile had a right to know. With the *Mordain* safely on its way Kennedy rose from the controls. As the other resumed his watch he added, "Weyburn sent for us. He didn't say just why, but I've the feeling there is trouble. Just what it is we'll find out when we arrive."

They saw it as the *Mordain* dropped from hydrive, the stars blurring to steady again as they fell below sub-C velocity, the bright points augmented by others, spots of flashing, glaring crimson, the warning beacons of a cluster of ships which surrounded something strange.

At the controls Chemile drew in his breath.

"Cap! What the hell is that?"

Kennedy leaned forward a little, concentrating on the screens, unable as yet to answer the question. The warning vessels contained a section of space which held a ring of turbulent luminescence, a thick torus of orange light that turned in and around itself in ceaseless motion. Within it, circled by the brilliance, lay nothing.

A void, an area as black as jet, nonreflective, the surface seeming to absorb all light as if it were a sponge, enigmatic and obviously dangerous.

The ships gave proof of that. The guardian patrol, the cloud of auxiliaries armed and watchful, the great bulk of the mother ship beyond. The full might of MALACA 1, the defensive force of Earth itself, the core and heart of Terran Control.

Commander Olsen was waiting at the port as the *Mordain* docked. A tall, tough, rangy man, his face seemed to be carved from teak, his eyes direct, his body rigid beneath the blue, green, and silver of his uniform.

"Cap!" His grip was firm. "It's good to see you again, though I wish it could have been under different circumstances. You saw it?"

Kennedy nodded. "What is it?"

"We don't know, and that's the trouble. We just don't know." Olsen hesitated as if about to say more and then deciding against it. "There's a meeting arranged in an hour. Weyburn is here and Harbin."

"Jud Harbin?" Kennedy frowned. If the Military Supremo of Terran Control had taken over direct command, then the situation had to be more than serious. "An hour, you say. Good. Can you arrange for the exchange and replenishment of supplies and armament?"

"Of course, Cap. The usual procedure." The hard face cracked into the ghost of a smile. "Though I hope that, this time, your engineer won't upset my technicians. I almost had a mutiny on my hands the last time he told them what he thought of them."

"Just ignore him," said Kennedy, though knowing it was an impossibility if the giant had set his mind against it. "And you'd better tell Jarl to join me. I've the feeling he may be wanted."

Weyburn and Harbin were not alone. Together with them at the table sat a small, balding man with a receding chin and a uniform which fitted only where it touched. He rose as Kennedy entered with Luden; his hand outstretched, his face beaming with pleasure.

"Professor Jarl Luden," he said. "This is indeed an honor. May I say what pleasure your paper on the Quendial Artifacts gave me? A pleasure doubled by your treatise on the Moomianian Scrolls. As a devoted student of the Zheltyana mystery I found them both of great help."

"Sit down, Corey." Harbin didn't raise his voice but his tone held the whiplash of command. "We have more important things to do than exchange mutual congratulations. Cap, you've seen that thing out there?"

"Yes."

"What did you think of it?"

"I've had no time to study it," Kennedy said dryly. "Can you tell me what it is?"

"No." Harbin squared his shoulders and Kennedy realized that he, like them all, was suffering from fatigue. Corey's eyes were too bright, a sign of drugs to stimulate his metabolism, and Weyburn, slumped in his chair, seemed to be dozing. An illusion, destroyed as he moved a little and opened his eyes.

"Get on with it, Jud."

Those five words established the real seat of command. Harbin controlled all Terran Forces, the mighty MALACAs that guarded the Terran Sphere, units capable of destroying worlds, their men and machines capable of resisting any invader. But half of the function of the Mobile Aid Laboratory and Construction Authorities was to create. To give aid to developing worlds. Yet the powers to destroy and to create were limited by the delicate balance of political power.

Weyburn worked in the dark. When normal diplomacy had failed and when the naked use of force could only result in desperate reprisals, then he came into his own. Like a spider at the center of a galaxy-wide web he directed his secret agents, the Free Acting Terran Envoys, each with tremendous responsibility, able to act as their own judge, jury, and executioner, to stamp out the fire of incipient war before it could blaze, to use any means at their command to maintain the *Pax Terra.*

And Kennedy was the foremost of this specially selected corps of men.

He said, "What is the background? When was the torus first seen? What tests have been made?"

Harbin cleared his throat. A glass of water stood before him and he sipped a little, setting down the glass with a decisive rap.

"This is what we know, Cap. Some prospectors took off for a point beyond Pluto. There were three of them, Elg Rowan, Neil Quimper, José Oveido. Oveido was a dreamer who though he had located a rogue planetoid. A wanderer. Quimper had money. Rowan had a ship. Together they set out to find this supposed bonanza."

Luden said, "Did they or is that just rumor?"

"Fact, Jarl; we've checked. On Ceres, at the Institute Companstola at Madrid, with the Dreux Feugert Finance Company in the Belt. Three hopefuls chasing a dream. An old story—but this time they found it. A call was received from Quimper, the routine notification of legal claim to a new discovery. He gave the coordinates, a description, and the usual relevant data. Apparently he had returned to the vessel for air and tools and wanted to be sure the claim was registered. Naturally we were interested. When we got a second call we were more than that. Listen to the recording."

A small machine stood on the table. At Harbin's gesture Corey touched a button. A thin, pain-racked voice filled the room.

Luden sighed as it ended. "They found something," he said. "An artifact of great complexity. The description is poor but it was obviously a machine of some kind. And then—?"

"Nothing." Harbin scowled. "A ship was sent out to make contact. It didn't find the three men and it didn't find the planetoid. Instead it found that!" His thumb jerked toward space, the mystery it contained. "And now we've got it in our laps."

Kennedy said quietly, "Literally?"

"Literally!" Harbin's hand slammed against the table. "That's what all this is about, Cap. Don't you understand? The damned thing is moving. Unless it is stopped it will intersect the orbit of Earth." He paused for a moment, and then added bitterly, "And intersect it at just the wrong time. Both it and the planet will arrive at the same point at the same time—and anything it touches vanishes as though it had never been."

CHAPTER THREE

For a long moment there was silence in which small sounds became suddenly loud; the scrape of a chair, Corey's sleeve rustling as he moved, a vibration as someone passed beyond the door, and another sound, odd in such a place, the faint but unmistakable rasp of claws.

Then Weyburn said, opening his eyes, "You've lived with this too long, Jud. You forget that Cap doesn't know what the hell you're talking about."

Kennedy's brain, quick with a natural intuition, had assessed the scant information and extrapolated it into a recognizable whole. Perhaps not the details but there had been no mistaking the strain behind the words, the acceptance of the inevitable should things stay as they were.

Something mysterious in space, born from an unknown machine, drifting on a course that would impact it against a densely populated world. He tried to remember the exact dimensions of the torus and failed. It had been small, that he remembered, far too small to engulf a planet, but that wouldn't be necessary. Not to insure complete destruction. If anything it touched vanished, then it would drill through the crust, into the magma below, releasing the buried fury of volcanic activity. And worse. A world penetrated by a shaft of destruction would end in catastrophe. Any world. And one which was a mesh of communications, industries, teeming cities, and carefully nurtured agricultural areas—

Kennedy became aware of Luden's thin, precise tones.

"I would suggest that we do not allow emotion to cloud our scientific evaluation of the threat. I take it that the course and velocity of the torus has been carefully calculated and that there is no possibility of error?"

"No, Jarl." Harbin was definite. "I've had the full rescources of MALACA 1 on the job together with all the outside talent willing to be engaged." He glanced at the small man. "Corey for one."

"Dr. Corey," said Luden stiffly. "Of, as I remember, the Kracow University."

"Professor! You have heard of me?"

"I must admit to a lapse of memory, Doctor, but you are not unknown. Did you supervise the measurements?"

"I was asked to conduct a separate investigation. As a reservist, you understand."

"To make a check, naturally. And your results matched that of the technicians? You allowed for galactic drift? Gravitational aberration? Magnetic influences? And Luna—would it impede the path of the torus?" Luden bobbed his head at each positive answer. "Then I think we can safely assume the facts as stated by the Supremo are correct. Providing, naturally, that nothing intervenes between now and the time of intersection. The next step is to anticipate what damage might be caused if Earth was impacted against the torus."

Kennedy said, "That doesn't matter, Jarl. Not at this time. Precautions can be taken but it will be impossible to evacuate the planet. What I'd like to know is what the hell has been done to stop it."

Harbin bridled. "You think we've been wasting our time?"

"Tell me."

"I've had ships fire megaton atomics at the torus without result. We've tried creating magnetic fields to alter its path—negative. We've some new tractor beams—useless. I've tried using various types of restraining mesh—we might as well have thrown cobwebs at the sun. You name it and we've tried it—all but one thing. As yet we haven't tried sending torpedoes through the ring."

"Why not?"

"Ask him." Harbin nodded toward Weyburn. "But we have tried a charge to be detonated at the moment of impact—negative. The thing simply drank the energy. In fact it seemed to grow larger so we stopped at once. We're in enough trouble as it is."

Weyburn said, "All right, Cap. You've heard the basics. Now tell me what conclusions you've drawn."

Kennedy doubted it was an appeal for help. The day Weyburn had to ask for help to make a decision would be the day he resigned as Director of Terran Control. A verification of his own suspicions then? Or perhaps he was asking, in an indirect way, for support of his own extrapolations.

He said, slowly, "Let us examine the facts as we know them. Some prospectors found a rogue planetoid, or rather not a rogue but one with a tremendously extended orbit. You have checked the figures?"

"As I told you," said Harbin dully. "Madrid has them on file."

"If Oveido found them, then so could others. Maybe the Chambodians or some other race who has no love for us. It is barely possible they built something on that mass of rock when it was way outside of the system. A bomb of sorts. Something which may have been accidentally triggered by Rowan and his friends. It would have been carried deep into the system and then, perhaps, have been detonated at a certain distance from the sun. It's a poor assumption, but let us consider it."

Corey said, surprisingly, "Negative. Too many assumptions have to be made. First that an enemy would know of the planetoid. That they have the technology to build such a device. That it would create devastation when detonated. That no one would investigate the rogue when it came into the system. Logic is against it."

"I agree." Luden nodded his approval.

"So we can discount that," continued Kennedy. "So what is left? An accident, a genuine one, or someone, somewhere, is trying—" He broke off. "Wait. Did the message give any indication of the age of that apparatus? Play the recording again."

"Old," he said when it had finished. "It has to be. Quimper mentioned that it was under the rock. Big, golden bars, an arrangement of units set in series to create a cascade of energy. He had some small scientific knowledge. Damn it, why didn't those fools leave it alone!"

Luden shared that regret.

"Cap! It could have been built by the Zheltyana! An operating artifact probably incorporating scientific principles unknown to us. Gone now," he mourned. "Totally lost. An opportunity to learn so much wantonly destroyed."

They were wandering from the point. Regret and speculation could come later, now an emergency had to be dealt with.

And he knew why Weyburn was reluctant to fire atomic missiles into the torus.

"You've tested it," said Kennedy. "You've passed material through it. What happened?"

Corey gave the answer.

"Very little. First we sent through a radio-slave probe. All contact was immediately lost. We tried another set on automatic return. Again negative. You realize that we sent several, that I speak in relative terms."

Kennedy said, curtly, "I assume that you know your job. And?"

"I made a personal series of tests. The movement of the torus was known so it was perfectly safe for me to ride ahead of it at a short distance from the curtain. I tried several things, a rod, a cable—I wanted to determine whether or not the curtain actually destroyed material or transmitted it. Whether or not it was in fact a door. A portal leading from here to—somewhere else. A wild assumption, perhaps, but I was curious."

Kennedy began to find him more courageous than he seemed. To hang suspended before a curtain which could easily snatch his life, to probe into it with short-range devices, to test a theory which was against all logic—

Kennedy looked at the little man with growing respect.

"And?"

"It is a portal," Corey said firmly. "A distortion of space which represents something equivalent to a black hole. I can describe it no better. But if someone, somewhere, had invented a means of instantaneous transmission, a matter-transmitter of scientific speculation, then I feel it would look very much like the torus. The movement too, is odd. Technically it should follow the path of the planetoid, but it does not. Therefore it seems to me to be a logical assumption that it is one end of, for convenience, let us call it a dimensional tunnel. One end here, moving; the other held fast somewhere else."

"Or both moving with the galactic drift," said Luden. "Which would mean that the portal, if it is that, must be stationary with respect to the galaxy." He added, "You have proof?"

"Yes," said Corey. "Sam."

Stooping, he lifted a basket from under the table. In it was a cat.

It was a big beast, a scarred tom, one ear torn, the other twitching, and Kennedy knew now from where the rasp of claws had come. Corey opened the basket and lifted it out, one hand stroking the thick, black fur.

"Sam," he said. "I had to find out if living things could penetrate the torus and remain unharmed. So I sealed him in a small probe attached to the end of a stiff rod. A very short rod, you understand. A long cable was sheared; it seems that any divergence breaks material at the line of penetration. Anyway, he went through and I pulled him back. Several times. As you can see he is unharmed."

Kennedy met Wayburn's eyes.

"People," he said. "Maybe another race beyond the torus. It could come out on a friendly world or a hostile one. Rumor travels fast, and if we sent missiles through and if they should explode and take out a planet?"

"Politics." Harbin echoed his disgust. "Always politics. To hell with others as long as Earth is saved."

He didn't mean it, having spoken from frustration, a safety valve for the constant strain of restraint, of walking on eggs, of remembering, always, that one wrong move, one thoughtless act could trigger galactic war.

Weyburn said, "That's it, Cap, in part at least. Harbin tells me the torus can't be stopped on this side. We know that life can pass through it unharmed. Maybe, if it can be stopped at all, it will have to be from the other side. I don't know, but we have to find out." He hesitated, and then slowly added, "And there's more—but you know what that is."

The thing could not be put into words before Corey. The need for a trained and experienced ambassador—or a tried and tested assassin. Kennedy was both. Weyburn trusted him to handle any situation he might find in the best possible way for Earth and the *Pax Terra.*

Harbin said gruffly, "I must tell you this, Cap. We've already sent one ship through. A small scout, three-man crew. They had orders to return immediately. They didn't."

"When?"

"As soon as Corey told us about his cat. Two days now."

"Maybe they didn't have Sam's luck," said Kennedy. Rising, he reached forward and stroked the arched back of the cat, which purred and batted his hand with a velvet paw. "Maybe I should take him with me."

"With us, Cap," Luden said firmly. "And we can't take the animal. You know how Veem feels about pets. To spite him Penza will pretend to hate the animal or get one of his own, and before we know it the *Mordain* will be like a menagerie. It will be worse than their present rivalry as to who can make the best coffee."

"All right, Jarl," said Kennedy. "The cat stays behind."

"A wise decision." Rising, Luden said to Corey, "It has been a pleasure meeting you, Doctor. One day, perhaps, we can continue our interrupted discussion on the subjects you mentioned. In the meantime, during our absence, I suggest that the path of the planetoid be scanned for any debris which may have been thrown clear of whatever happened. There could be fragments, perhaps, of inestimable value to science."

From the bridge Harbin and Weyburn watched them go. Small on the screens the *Mordain* turned, aiming, drifting a little before moving steadily toward the center of the torus at a mounting velocity.

"Let's hope they have better luck than the others." Olsen flipped a switch. "I insisted they maintain continuous radio contact. Listen."

From the speaker came a droning monotone, Luden's voice, dry, dispassionate.

"We will hit at a high velocity, both to minimize the shock of transference and to lessen the danger of impacting the inner sides of the torus. We have adopted battle stations. I shall now play a recording of music as my attention must be concentrated on the matter at hand. On second thought, correct that. No music. It will be a distraction. Instead, despite your order, I shall resume contact the moment we have passed through."

"Belay that!" snapped Olsen. "Keep talking."

"Very well. We are now very close . . ."

The voice droned on as they watched the *Mordain* gain speed, darting between the auxiliaries, the warning ships, lancing like an arrow to hit at the dead center of the torus.

The droning voice died as if cut with a knife.

Harbin drew a ragged breath. "The same," he muttered. "Just like the others. Damn you, Elias! Cap was one of the best."

"I know that, Jud."

"Then why—oh, hell!"

Weyburn made no comment, standing, staring at the screen, hoping that the voice would return yet knowing that it wouldn't, that there was nothing now to do but wait, and wait, and wait.

When he finally turned from the screen he looked very old.

CHAPTER FOUR

It was like a flash, a blink, the wink of an eye. One moment they were hurtling toward the torus and then they were through, the orange ring falling behind as Luden's voice came over the speakers.

"Contact broken, Cap. No response from MALACA 1."

Kennedy had expected it. What he hadn't expected was the utter normality of the space in which he found himself. The stars looked the same, the fuzz of distant nebulas, even the sun which glowed small on the screens. A different sun, of course; it had to be. As this had to be a different space. A part of the normal universe, perhaps, but somewhere remote from Earth.

Chemile's voice came from the turret. "Cap! A ship!"

Kennedy had already seen it, a small, familiar shape bearing familiar markings. The scout from MALACA 1 drifted in the void, the side ripped, metal burned, the edges twisted and fused by intense heat.

Something else loomed huge and close. It was a ball ridged and spined with protrusions, with slender needles tipped and ringed with lambent green.

The wrecked scout saved them. The fraction of warning it had given had been enough, that and the shelter offered by its small bulk. Even as emerald fire blazed from the alien vessel Kennedy was reacting by trained instinct, moving the *Mordain* without the hampering need of conscious thought, the vessel a living extension of his own body.

As livid shafts of green seared the void where they had been the *Mordain* darted to the side of the scout

34

opposite the spined ball. The little vessel glowed from the impact of savage energies, metal fusing, vaporizing, the hull limned in a nimbus of emerald light, a protective barrier which Kennedy used as he sent the *Mordain* streaking away, voice hard as he snapped orders to Chemile at the guns.

"Get it, Veem! Fast!"

They were too close for torpedoes; their atomic fury would be as dangerous to the *Mordain* as to the alien bulk from which emerald fire lanced in spears of radiant energy. Kennedy dodged them, hands tight on the controls, eyes narrowed, calculating, gauging time and distance.

"Now, Veem!"

The order was unnecessary, already Chemile had fired, the heavy-duty Dione mounted in the turret blasting its shaft of raw destruction. A handgun could sear a hole through a man; the one they carried could puddle a large house into molten slag at a single shot.

Plates glowed white-hot where it struck, a turret puffing into vapor, slender needles sagging, wreathed with eroding energy. Again the Dione fired, and then Kennedy threw them up and away, feeling the jar as emerald flame reached out to touch the hull.

"Jarl?"

"Minor damage, Cap. Our shield absorbed most of the energy."

"Maintain full protective power, Penza."

"Will do, Cap." Saratov was calm. "Why not blast it with the torps?"

A temptation. The *Mordain* was the fastest vessel in normal space, already they were far from the alien hulk, and it would be simple to destroy it with atomic might. But if they did the destruction would be complete, and there was much Kennedy hoped to learn.

And there was a complication.

"Jarl, check the screens. I see no sign of that vessel."

"The screens are operational, Cap. That vessel must have a protective baffle of some kind." He paused, busy with his instruments, then added, "Nothing conclusive, but we can make a logical assumption. It seems obvious that it could have a deflection field operating on a wide range of the electromagnetic spectrum. A means to rotate light and other radiation in a one hundred and eighty degree arc so that when we look at the vessel we actually see what lies beyond it."

Or perhaps it carried a means of travel impossibly efficient, a drive which could move it so fast that, in the wink of an eye, it had passed beyond the range of the detectors.

Kennedy touched the controls, the stars blurring as they reached and passed the speed of light to almost immediately blur and steady again as he dropped from hydrive. He repeated the protective maneuver, as he flung the *Mordain* back toward the orange ring of the torus, the tiny shape of the wrecked scout which still glowed with an emerald haze.

And the alien ship was before them.

It sprang from nothingness, abrupt against the stars, needles moving, green fire spouting, reaching, missing as Kennedy dodged, as Chemile again fired the Dione.

As the livid blast impacted the rounded hull, spreading in a white-hot glow, he triggered the large-caliber sprom cannon, a stream of self-propelled missiles tearing at the softened metal, ripping into it, rending it wide as the shells vented their stored energy in vicious explosions.

More shells struck the protrusions, the turrets that held the menacing needles, the hail of fire accompanied by intermittent blasts of the Dione. For a few moments the *Mordain* hung close to the alien hulk, quivering with the transmitted thunder of continuous fire, blasting the enemy weapons before they could come to bear, smashing down the opposition by the savage fury of a close-range attack.

The attack continued as Kennedy swung the *Mordain* from its position, veering the craft in a random escape pattern as Chemile maintained the fire on the cannon, throwing a hail of self-propelled missiles into the gaping hole torn in the alien hull.

And, this time, it did not vanish.

It hung, the needles still, the lambent green fire which had tipped and ringed them dead as the entire vessel was dead, a mass of metal, its mechanisms destroyed, any life it contained incapable of further resistance.

Alert, keyed for instant action, Kennedy edged the *Mordain* closer to the gaping hole the guns had torn in the plates.

"Cap?" Chemile's voice was uneasy. "Are we going in?"

"We need information, Veem. This vessel could give us some."

"It contained no air," said Luden. "I was watching closely all through the attack. There was no escape of vapor. Of course the crew could have been suited and fought in a vacuum. Unusual, but perhaps the offensive mechanisms operated better under such conditions. In that case the hull could still hold operational units capable of destruction."

"Come up and take over the controls, Jarl. Veem, keep a close watch. Take evasive action if attacked."

"If you're going in there, Cap, then I'm coming with you." Saratov's deep rumble left no room for argument. "I'm suiting up now."

Together they kicked free of the *Mordain*, drifting toward the alien hulk, gekko-boots holding them fast on the ruptured hull. Cautiously they eased through the opening, Diones ready in gloved hands, helmets-beams glinting on a tangle of shattered equipment.

Saratov said, wonderingly, "This is weird, Cap. The construction is crazy. Where are the bulkheads? The compartments? The whole thing seems to be just a ball filled with equipment."

The conclusion was fast but correct. A normal vessel would have held men, supplies, air for them to breathe, places where they could rest. As they roved through the ship Kennedy found none of these things. No men, no bodies, nothing which told of the presence of life of any kind.

"A robot," said Luden. He had joined them after an hour, when it was certain the wrecked vessel held no threat. "A self-contained automatically operating mechanism. It accounts for the lack of air, of course, machines have no need to breathe and, in fact, electronic apparatus works better in a vacuum. But there has to be a central computer of some kind."

It rested at the center of the hull, a casing which had split open beneath the impact of a shell to reveal a mass of apparatus and something which oozed a pale gray and red.

"A cyborg control." Saratov's voice held disgust. "A living brain hooked into a life-support apparatus and connected to the circuits of the ship. Human, Jarl?"

Luden bent close, his light bright on the fragile remains, one gloved hand lifting, touching.

"It's difficult to tell, Penza," he said precisely. "But the size and convolutions resemble that of a human brain. There are, of course, other races with craniums as large as ours, animals also, the dolphins for example, but from what I can make out of the cerebrum, yes, this is a human brain."

Taken from its body, it was fitted with pipes and extensions, given a horrible travesty of life so that conscious and aware it had lain trapped in a living hell. What manner of culture had done this? And why?

Back in the *Mordain* Luden said thoughtfully, "We can make certain extrapolations from what we have learned, Cap. The fort could have been one of a number scattered throughout this space on constant watch or it could have been placed to destroy anything which came through the torus. I am inclined to think the former is the case. If the latter I think it reasonable to expect more than one vessel and certainly an investigation team of some kind."

"So we were just unlucky," boomed Saratov. "But not as unlucky as that scout. They must have been burned before they knew it." Frowning, he added, "A pity we wrecked it so badly. I would have liked to examine that baffle they must have used."

"We can overcome it, Penza. A mass-detector fitted to the screens working in conjunction with the normal detection apparatus will do it." Luden dismissed the problem with a gesture. "I feel that the use of the cyborg is of greater importance at the moment. It is clear proof of the existence of a society with a high level of technological achievement coupled with a distorted value of life."

"Cyborgs aren't unknown, Jarl," said Kennedy. "The Vilkar use them."

"True, Cap, but under stringent control. The most debased of criminals, the hoplessly crippled if they give their permission, some scientists who accept the loss of normal bodily function in order to extend their mental existence to continue their studies."

"So they claim," grunted Saratov. "Personally I'm not so sure. I've heard some nasty stories about the Vilkar. The quicker we do something about it the better."

"Perhaps, Penza," Luden said dryly. "But that problem has no place in the present situation. We have more immediate needs."

To check the space they were in, to find a habitable world, to find some means of destroying the torus. And to move away from a position of probable danger.

Kennedy sent the *Mordain* hurtling toward the sun. Spectroscopic analysis would perhaps identify it and place them in a known region if they were still in the normal universe. As it grew larger in the screens a nagging sense of something wrong itched at his consciousness. It was too familiar. He had seen something like it too often before.

"Cap!" Luden's voice held a strained disbelief. "I've checked the sun. It's a yellow G-type and it's identical to Sol."

"And?"

Luden had conducted the obvious checks.

"I've taken sights on five stars at selected points, Cap. The constellations match those as seen from the solar system and the spectrographs of Rigel, Deneb, Sirius, Polaris, and Aldebaran are exactly the same as those in our own universe. There can be no doubt, Cap. We haven't moved in space at all!"

Kennedy stared bleakly at the screens, remembering the sun they had left behind them when they had entered the torus, the sun which had lain ahead after they had passed through. The same sun but in another direction. Somehow they had turned a full 180 degrees—but it had to be more than that. The ships of MALACA 1 had vanished to be replaced with an alien artifact, the fort which they had destroyed. And if the immediate region of space had altered, then so must other things. Despite the evidence they could not be in familiar surroundings.

Before him the screens flashed red, the blast of the alarm following the visual signal. It died as he hit the cutoff, Chemile's yell sounding almost as loud. "Cap! Trouble!"

It came from three directions at once, lambent green fire circling the tapering bases of slender shapes, vessels like sharks, long, narrow, vicious, summoned perhaps by a message from the destroyed fort, arrowing in for the kill.

They fell away as Kennedy fed power to the drive, reaching and passing plus-C velocity as he sent the *Mordain* high above the plane of the ecliptic. Again the screen flared as more vessels registered their presence, squat this time, spined, winking out of existence as fast as they had appeared. But there would be more, thicker as he neared the sun, a multi-ringed defense against which he had only one sure weapon, the speed of the *Mordain*.

The speed brought the ship to a point above the third planet from the sun. The world which had to be Earth.

The moon blurred, steadied as Kennedy cut velocity, passed as he fell toward the mottled green, brown, and blue ball traced with fleecy white clouds blotched with menacing shapes. Orbiting forts of peculiar construction, treble cones joined at the bases to form three-pointed stars. Fire blasted from one, a thick finger of green flame, and Kennedy felt the *Mordain* jerk to the impact of violent energies. Skillfully he maintained control, moving too fast for safety, taking a desperate gamble as he ran the gauntlet of the orbiting vessels.

If he could hit an ocean, drop beneath the surface, and hide under the polar ice there would be time to think and plan. Or, if not an ocean, some mountainous region in which the ship could be hidden under a covering of stone.

The alarm sounded again, red flashes appearing on the screens, overlaying the blur of ground which rose too fast, the rounded shapes which hung too thickly. Sound blasted through the vessel as something hit the hull to explode with shattering fury. Air whined through a torn plate, turbulence fighting the controls as Kennedy cut velocity, causing the *Mordain* to veer and swing toward a range of jagged peaks tipped with snow, valleys filled with trees which bent beneath the wind of their passing.

"Veem! Ready a torp. Three-second fuse. Aim as directed."

"Right, Cap."

Kennedy tensed as the ground flashed close. Their speed was too great, to land now would be to leave a trail leading directly to where they would be hidden. And yet he dared not wait much longer. A lake appeared, a patch of blue water which passed to be replaced by another. A low hill of naked stone.

"Veem! That hill. Fire!"

He hit the lake as the torpedo exploded, atomic fire gouging into the stone, shattering the hill, sending up a thick column of smoke and vapor. Water flumed, the dragging impact slowing the ship to rest as it sank beneath the surface, more water gushing in through the hole torn in the hull.

"Cap!" Drenched, Saratov staggered through the bulkhead and slammed the airtight door. He was hurt, blood running from a wound on one arm, his face blackened. "Cap?"

"I'm all right, Penza." Kennedy turned from the controls. "Veem? Jarl?"

They gathered in the control room, tense as they waited, watching the telltales, the instruments relaying movement above.

As they stilled Kennedy relaxed. The desperate gamble had been won. The torpedo fired against the hill had covered their landing, giving the impression that the *Mordain* had crashed and disintegrated into ruin, the debris it had scattered covering the lake and surrounding area and destroying all trace of the hidden vessel.

If nothing else they had at least gained time.

CHAPTER FIVE

Luden reached for a hypogun, blasted an anesthetic drug into Saratov's bloodstream, waited a moment, then picked up a probe.

"You've got a fragment of metal in that arm," he said. "Now hold still, Penza, while I take it out."

"You could have done it without the anesthetic, Jarl," rumbled the giant. "I'm not like Veem. I don't scream at a scratch."

"I heard that," snapped Chemile from where he stood in the galley. "If you want some of this coffee you'd better watch your tongue. Anyway, Jarl, isn't it true that morons have a naturally low pain level?"

"Meaning?" Saratov tried to rise from the table, grunted as Luden impatiently thrust him down. "Cap, do you think I'm an idiot?"

"You will be if you don't lie still." Kennedy watched as Luden lifted a jagged fragment from the wound. "Serious damage, Jarl?"

"No, as usual Penza was lucky. He might be sore for a while but that's all." Luden skillfully dressed the wound after injecting a hormone compound to promote rapid healing. "Now let me look at that face."

The blackness was superficial, powder stains from the explosives that had torn the hull. Washed, a cup of coffee in his big hand, the giant looked as good as new.

"The ship's a mess, Cap," he said ruefully. "We'll have to patch the hull and pump out that water before we can even start to repair the damage. Whatever hit us on the way down played hell with the compensators."

"It was a satellite bomb," said Chemile. "The air was thick with them. Or maybe it was an aircar."

"It was a bomb," said Luden. "One containing chemical explosives, fortunately, or Penza would be dead now. But I think he is referring to the green energy which struck us from that triple-coned fort. A most unusual weapon; it seems to distort the normal gravitation exchange in stable matter into a self-destructive turbulence. Not as efficient, I would say, as our own means of destruction, but interesting in its application of a little known principle."

Kennedy said dryly, "I would have appreciated it far more, Jarl, if we hadn't been on the receiving end."

"True, Cap, but the use of gravitons in such a manner gives rise to speculation. It would be tempting to see if a shield could not be developed against it, perhaps by the use of a heterodyning field of some kind. If so—"

"Later, Jarl," Kennedy interrupted firmly. Setting down his empty cup, he said, "On the way down did anyone see anything? You, Veem?"

"I was pretty busy," said Chemile. "But I did notice that there was no space complex at the Andes."

"Neither was there any sign of the Sahara Reclamation," said Luden. "Most of the coast of North Africa was complete desert."

"And the Siberian Solar Station was missing." Saratov frowned. "If this is Earth, Cap, then it's changed a hell of a lot since I was here last."

"It isn't Earth," said Kennedy. "At least not the Earth we know. The orbiting forts tell us that and since when did we have satellite bombs? A time warp, Jarl?"

"It is possible, Cap," admitted Luden. "After all, we know nothing about the torus except that it abruptly appeared. Yet some things cannot be argued against. The sun for one. There is no doubt that it is Sol. That this area of space is the solar system and that this planet is Earth. However, it is not the planet we know, so there are three obvious conclusions. We either traveled far into the past or into the future. If into the past, then I would expect to see a totally different environment, certainly not a highly developed civilization. If into the future, then the race must have regressed—

the use of the cyborg tells us that. However, it seems the most logical conclusion to draw from the available evidence, which, as yet, is very limited."

"A regression," said Chemile. "But how long would such a thing take, Jarl? How far are we in the future?"

"If we are in the future, Veem," Luden corrected. "And it would not take long for the society we know to degenerate given one or more basic premises. For example there could have been a disastrous war. Or the moral fiber could have been eroded by, say the introduction of a new narcotic. Or there could have been some natural catastrophe which destroyed civilization or so badly disrupted it that it was unable to regain its previous eminence."

The torus, perhaps? Kennedy visualized again the devastation it would cause should it impact with the planet. The destruction would be immense and the shattered world would be a prey to outside forces. Envious combines would snatch at the worlds allied to Terran Control, and even if the guardian MALACAs should spread retribution the erosion would continue. Without the brain the body could not survive.

Had he seen what would be left? A world turned into a place guarded by rings of ships and bombs? A solitary planet turning to cyborg slavery in order to maintain its technology?

How long would such regression take?

Not long, that he knew all too well. A few decades could distort growth for all time. A hundred years set a destructive pattern. A thousand, and even the memory of a gentler culture would become a vague legend.

And, if this was the future, how could it be changed?

Harshly he said, "The third conclusion, Jarl? An alternative world?"

"Yes, Cap. A remote possibility, but theoretically a viable one. Certainly the torus moved us, and we know that it didn't do it in terms of distance. It could have done it in terms of time, but if not, then it must have done it in terms of alternate space."

"Wait a minute, Jarl." Saratov rubbed at his arm,

frowning. "I know of the theory of alternate existence, of course, but let me get it straight. You think we might have passed through the torus into a space exactly like our own in terms of physical reference, but different in terms of evolution. Right?"

Kennedy said, before Luden could answer, "Think of it this way, Penza. Imagine a universe to be a page in a book and also imagine there are an infinity of pages. They are all exactly alike aside from the printing on them. We belong to one page, the printing is our history, the smallest details of the entire universe. The next page will be a little different; for example we could all be here just as we are now but you would have hair and Veem could be, say, three feet tall. And so it goes on, each universe different from the others."

"And the torus provided a gate so that we could move from one universe or page to another." Chemile nodded. "I get it. So all we have to do to get back home is to pass through the torus from this side. Well, it's nice to know we aren't stuck."

Luden cleared his throat. "It isn't as simple as that, Veem. We have no assurance that we shall return to our own space at all. The theory of a black hole, for example, is that it would be impossible to return. Always we would arrive at a totally different universe."

Kennedy said quietly, "Jarl, you're forgetting Sam."

"Sam?"

"The cat, Jarl. Corey's cat. It went through and it came back."

"I'd forgotten," Luden admitted. "Veem, my apologies, I have caused you unnecessary concern. As you say all we have to do to get back home is to pass through the torus again."

"If we can," said Saratov grimly. "There are a lot of ships that may want to stop us. And the condition the *Mordain*'s in we couldn't even lift out of this water, let alone make it into space." It was an exaggeration, but too close to the truth for comfort.

After the hull was sealed and the compartment

drained Kennedy watched as the giant made a detailed examination.

"Well, Penza?"

"We can lift, Cap, but only just. We can make space but the hydrive is out and will stay that way until I rebuild the compensator. That isn't going to be easy. From the look of it I'll need a new set of crystals and it's a fair bet the coils are out of tune." He slammed one meaty fist against the soiled hump of the engine. "Damn that fort! We were doing fine until it hit us."

"Just what do you need?"

"A new engine, Cap, but that's impossible. I'll have to retune the coils as best I can." Restlessly the giant paced the engine room, pausing to touch, to examine, finally managing to relax a little. Calmer now, he said, "Most of the replacements can be got from the spares or other equipment, but that green blast disintegrated the main compensator node and it will have to be replaced if we hope to move at more than a few G's of acceleration."

"But we can travel without it?"

"Yes, Cap, we can." Saratov was grim. "But what chance would we have against the forts and other vessels if we can't maneuver?"

None. To even attempt it would be suicide, Kennedy knew. Without the compensator to nullify inertial strain they would be crushed to a pulp; even the giant's incredible strength would be unable to withstand the excessive gravitational force generated by the high accelerations needed to fight in space.

Kennedy said decisively, "We need a large crystal of zirnalite or an acceptable alternative and there's only one way we can get it. In any case we need information about this world. Facts to help us to destroy the torus, and equipment."

"It's a risk, Cap," said Luden. "We don't know if we are in the past or future of our own world or if we are in a totally different one. We don't know local customs or regulations. We have no idea, even, just where we are." He paused, frowning, studying the problem as if it were a specimen beneath his microscope. "As I remember there were mountains to the north. They will make progress difficult and it is unlikely that any center of industry will lie in that immediate direction. It would be best to head south. We shall need certain items of equipment, some food and water, weapons, something to use as barter."

"And communicators," Saratov said decisively. "Transceivers incorporating a location device so that you can find the *Mordain*. Veem, make some more coffee! We've work to do!"

They left at dawn, rising through the water to swim to the southern edge of the lake, there to don clothing which had been kept dry in plastic bags. Luden shivered a little as he dressed, his thin frame sensitive to the cold. Kennedy handed him a needler, slipping its twin beneath his shirt. Lifting his wrist, he spoke softly into the apparent chronometer he wore on a thick band. Luden wore another.

"Checking, Penza. We're ready to go. How is reception?"

The giant's voice whispered from the dial like the hum of a trapped insect. "Good, Cap. How is the locator?"

Kennedy touched a stud and on the face of the chronometer a red point, minutely elongated, glowed against the dark background. As they moved from the vessel it would elongate into an arrow always aimed at where the ship was to be found.

"Fine."

"Jarl's also?"

Kennedy glanced to where Luden was checking his own instrument. "Yes. We're on our way."

"Luck, Cap."

A narrow path led from the edge of the lake, a game trail that wound through masses of dense vegetation. Kennedy led the way along it, his senses alert, eyes flickering from side to side, body tense for any danger. A rabbit darted across the path almost at his feet, and from a clump of bush, feathered objects rose to thresh the air with brownish wings.

The day warmed as they progressed, the ground rising, the air filling with the soft murmur of insects, the trilling song of birds. Trees reared tall around them, conifers that scented the air with the tang of pine, slim gray bodies racing up the boles to merge into the bark and watch with cautious squirrel eyes.

Underbrush rustled, a dry twig snapping with a sharp report, and a deer broke cover and darted before them, antlered head held high. The beast was followed by a doe and a pair of fawns, their speckled coats blurring their outlines as they vanished in the bushes.

Kennedy halted, one hand on the needler, his eyes searching the woods from which the animals had come.

"Cap?" Luden's question was a whisper.

"Something startled those animals, Jarl."

"Us, perhaps?"

Kennedy shook his head. He had walked with a trained woodsman's skill, avoiding leaves that could rustle, twigs that could snap. Luden had followed in his exact path, the pair of them drifting like ghosts.

Cautiously Kennedy stepped forward again, conscious of the primitive warnings of danger, the tension at the back of his neck, the rigidity of stomach muscles, released adrenaline which accelerated the beat of his heart.

Something was in the forest and it was stalking them.

A small clearing opened among the trees, edged with a mass of broken stone, boulders worn and coated with a fuzz of lichen. From a point to the right birds rose in a sudden explosion of wings, wheeling to rise in tight formation, to vanish among a screen of branches. The thrum of their wings was echoed by a coughing roar.

The cougar sprang.

It came from the edge of rocks, a savagely magnificent beast, cat-mask wreathed in a snarl, fangs gleaming in its parted jaws, limbs extended, paws reaching, the naked claws like needle-tipped sickles.

Kennedy moved, his shoulder slamming hard against

Luden, dropping to one knee, the needler lifting, aiming, firing as he pressed the trigger. Metallic darts sprouted on the furred chest and, in midair, the beast went limp, one back leg hitting Kennedy as it fell, the blow knocking him to one side.

"Cap!" Luden rose from where he had been thrown clear. "Are you hurt?"

"No."

Rising, Kennedy moved toward the cougar. It was unconscious, the anesthetic with which the darts were loaded having instant effect. As he drew them out he looked at the coat, the claws and fangs, the prominent ribs.

"It's wild, Jarl, and hungry."

This would be expected on a primitive world but not on the Earth he had known. There rare animals were safeguarded in open zoos, tended, monitored for any sickness, their environment softened by regular supplies of food.

"This could be a wildlife preserve, Cap," Luden said thoughtfully. "It would account for the absence of cabins around the lake. If so, the only people we are likely to find are wardens. Even so they should have lodges, probably beyond these hills and in more open ground."

They pressed on, the ground falling to a gentle slope, the trees thinning, yielding to tall grass and patches of bush, oaks now among the conifers, dense copses darkly green against the sky.

They thickened into a wood dotted with clearings, long avenues laced with slender branches that threw abstract patterns of shadow. At a place where two of the avenues intersected they found the body of a man.

He was naked, gaunt, ribs stark against the skin of his chest. He hung suspended from a wire rope that had buried itself so deeply into his throat that the coils could not be seen beneath the bulging flesh. His feet were scarred and thick with callouses. The hands were like incurved claws, the tips of the fingers blackly charred with fire. The back and flanks carried the thin mesh of cuts caused by a whip.

He had been dead, Kennedy knew, for only a few hours.

"Tortured," Luden whispered softly. "Whipped, then burned, then hanged. Left here, perhaps, as a warning to others." He turned as something rustled to the left, a rustle that was repeated to the right, at the rear. "Cap?"

"Don't move, Jarl," Kennedy said quietly. He too had heard the rustle and had caught a glimpse of movement. Lithe, painted figures invisible until they stirred. "Don't go for your gun or make any sudden gesture. We're surrounded."

Bleakly he looked at the dead man, the tilted face and the staring eyes, dull now in death but still seeming to hold an overwhelming terror.

A dead man left, not as a warning as Luden had assumed, but as bait in a trap that had snapped shut around them.

CHAPTER SIX

Natalie Toluca was bored. The hunt had been a mistake from the beginning and the thing which had fallen from the skies the previous day had effectively scared off all game. Three days wasted already and more to come. A week in which she was supposed to remain idle while others plotted and schemed. The Melford-Phrindah amalgamation would go through unopposed; a mistake but one she could no longer oppose. Tana Golchika would be spinning her web to lift her favorites to positions of power. Helen Estaler, always a weakling, would be falling even deeper into the snares of the Hitachi-Olmouta.

And her consort didn't help.

She looked sourly at where he sat, the soft light filtering through the fabric of the pavilion giving his face a blurred softness, his carefully tended hair a glow of muted crimson. He was busy with a map, dividers, some aerial photographs. A child playing with his toys, stubbornly refusing to accept the obvious.

Her voice held the snap of impatience. "Must you waste your time like that? Is there nothing better you could do?"

Royce Denholm looked up from the papers scattered on the small table. His face was smooth, almost devoid of character, the lips a little too full, the eyes a little too close. His voice matched the features, soft, bland, an expressionless combination of sounds.

"I thought we could make an investigation, my dear. It wouldn't take long. Traveling slowly we could reach the site of impact by tomorrow."

He was a man and therefore a fool. Acidly she said, "An aircar could reach it in an hour."

"True, but—"

"There is no need," she interrupted curtly. "An aerial survey has settled the matter. The object was a meteorite which disintegrated on impact. There can be no doubt as to the conclusion."

He was stubborn. "True, my dear, but there could be fragments that the aircars overlooked. My calculations show that there is an anomaly. If the object was a meteor then it was traveling far slower than it should have done and—"

"If?" Almost she was amused. "You consider that you are more qualified than Aerial Command to make a judgment?"

"No, my dear, but it seems to me that it would pay to make a fuller investigation. At least we could make a ground-search. If nothing else the trip would be good for the both of us. You work too hard and you know the doctors said you should learn to relax. That is why they suggested this vacation. We could travel slowly, porters could carry you in a litter if you wish."

Coldly she snapped, "I am not a cripple and neither am I too old to walk, but what you suggest is ridiculous. If I wanted to visit the site of impact I would naturally use an aircar, but such a journey would serve no purpose. Now put away your toys."

For a moment she thought he would refuse as he sat, rigid at the small table, and she felt a momentary exhilaration at the prospect of defiance. Then he yielded, hands trembling a little as he folded the map, stacked it together with the photographs and dividers.

Bleakly he said, "Do I annoy you, Natalie?"

A stupid question—he always annoyed her. It had been a mistake to have taken him as her consort in the first place, but political necessity had dictated the action, and at first he had at least been bearable. But then his intrusion into her affairs had ceased to be more than a minor irritation and had become an outright nuisance. There had been a confrontation and she warmed to the memory of it. The victory had been small and inevitable, but even so it had been a victory. Now, having been put firmly in his place, Royce was little more than a fashionable appendage.

And one which could be severed whenever she so decided.

Leaning back, she clapped her hands, and to the servant who appeared with quiet deference, she snapped, "Wine."

It held the familiar tang of medicines and she sipped it with little pleasure. The doctors had been right, damn them. She really should learn to relax. And yet it was hard to follow their instructions. There was too much to do, too many things were slipping from her control. The Nord-Am Quadrant was under both commercial and political attack. Already too many concessions had been made and more would follow if Helen Estaler couldn't be stopped. Her involvement with the Hitachi-Olmouta was dangerous and it was time the rest of the Council realized it. Tana Golchika, blinded by dreams of personal advantage, seemed unable to grasp the long-term implications of what she did. And there were others, too many others.

Why did she have to fight alone?

She looked over the rim of the half-empty goblet at Royce. Already the medication was taking effect; now she could look at him with detachment, free of the reactive irritation he too often caused. Perhaps she should have let him have his way. It would do little harm to allow him the use of porters and guards, and, perhaps, if she went with him, some amusement could be obtained.

Relaxed, eyes half closed, she drifted back in time when they had first met, he the sycophant of Guirda Han, she, unattached for the moment, intent on obtaining the woman's aid.

The price had been to make Royce her consort.

At the time she had thought him to be no more than a favored pet, his mistress seeking to find him a safe refuge—later she hadn't been so sure. There had been a mystery about Guirda Han—ugly rumors that associated her with something vile. Those rumors may have led to her suicide. If it had been suicide. Often Natalie wondered if it had been an assassin's hand that had held her under the water in the bath in which she had drowned. The pills found beside the tub were perhaps a planted excuse for the coma into which she was assumed to have fallen.

Well, no matter, she was dead and gone now and her secret with her. But Royce remained.

A gentle person, that she had to admit. With velvet hands and a knowing technique that had once thrilled her and could possibly do so again if ever she gave him the opportunity to try.

She felt her body begin to respond to half-forgotten memories and, startled, looked at her wine.

Had the medication formula been changed? Had subtle aphrodisiacs been added to augment the tranquilizing compound? Had Royce even—but no, he would never have dared. Such things were whispered of in the lower echelons, the subject of sniggering mirth. Men who had used devious means to gain influence and power, playing on age-old female weakness. But the women so influenced were fools, and she was not of their number.

Abruptly she felt the need of air.

Outside the pavilion it was warm, the sun bright on the cluster of tents which formed the camp, the sward a soft coat of emerald. Porters moved deftly about their tasks, polishing the already gleaming aircar, some busy over an open fire as they cooked their afternoon meal. Against the grass they looked drab, brown denim untouched by color muffling their bodies.

"My dear."

Royce was at her side, pointing. From the trees edging the clearing a small party was heading toward them. A group of Wardens—and something else.

"What is it?" She looked, frowning. "Strangers?"

The frown deepened as they came closer; then they

halted a few feet from where she stood. One of the Wardens, almost grotesque in his paint, saluted.

"We found them where the Freeman was hanging, my lady. We were keeping watch in case others of his tribe tried to remove the body."

"Are you still maintaining watch?"

"Of course, my lady. It is a pity the man died before he could reveal to us the whereabouts of their hide, but we shall find it, my lady, given time."

"You had better." Her voice was cold. "The reserve is not for the protection of such scum. Too easily they seem to find sanctuary here. I am almost tempted to think they have friends within your number."

"Impossible, my lady!" The Warden sweated beneath his camouflaging paint. "We are loyal to the Council."

"See that you remain so."

Dismissed, the man fell back as Natalie Toluca studied what they had found. Two men, one old, his lined face at variance with the bright touches of color on his clothing. She frowned at that; it was an anomaly, men who wished to remain hidden did not wear bright colors, and the clothing, too, was unusual, of a cut and style unknown to her.

The other?

Tall, she thought, so very tall, and that face, so very strong. Her eyes clung to it, almost as if feeding on the firm contours, the eyes hard and direct, the ridge of the jaw, and the lips which she knew could smile with tenderness or turn cruel. The body matched the face, hard, firm, wide shoulders sloping to a narrow waist, the stomach flat, the thighs long, smooth mounds of muscle. The clothing was somber, black edged with gold, devoid of insignia or adornment, but the man needed neither. What he was, radiated from him with an almost tangible intensity, firmness, determination, a ruthless insistence. She felt herself diminished a little. Here was a man of a type she had never known; one accustomed to command, the use of authority.

She said harshly, "Who are you?"

"Travelers," Kennedy said easily. "We are in distress and would appreciate your aid."

He studied her as she had studied him, seeing a tall, almost angular woman, her hair cropped to a golden helmet that framed a strong-boned, strong-jawed face. Her nose was a little too large, a fault compensated for by her eyes, which were large, widely-spaced, a vivid blue beneath thick, arching brows. Early middle-age he guessed, well-preserved with a body that would have been more attractive had it carried more fat to round the curves. She wore a crimson tunic crusted with gold braid and heavy with insignia. Pants of the same color were thrust into boots gleaming like polished jet.

Against her the man looked dull. He was a little younger, girlish in his slimness, wearing dark brown relieved with touches of crimson, the insignia she wore repeated in a broad circle on the upper left-hand breast.

"My name is Royce Denholm and I am consort to the lady Natalie Toluca who stands before you. She is a member of the Nord-Am Council. And you?" He frowned at the answer. "Luden? Kennedy? Is that all?"

"Isn't it enough?" Kennedy was cautious, aware that he was treading on dangerous ground. He had learned a little: Wardens guarded the preserve and hunted men as much as animals; Freemen ran—but from what? Criminals, perhaps, or social misfits of some kind. And the woman was obviously in command.

She said coldly, "What is your House? Who is your mistress?"

"We belong to the House of Fren," said Kennedy without hesitation. "Our mistress is the Lady Selene Var. If you aid us I am certain that she will be most grateful."

"Fren?" She frowned, thinking. "I have never heard of it and neither do I know a Selene Var."

Kennedy shrugged, deliberately casual. "The world is wide, my lady."

Natalie was conscious of a growing unease, not unconnected with the tall figure. He did not have the appearance of an assassin, and yet how could she be sure? Had she been advised—almost forced, now that she came to think about it—to go on this stupid hunt so that, away from her usual protection, she would make a more easily acceptable target?

"I think you are spies," she said abruptly. "From where? Nord-Chin? Sud-Af? Answer! I demand to know!"

From her side Royce said quickly, "How did you get here? An aircar?"

Kennedy saw the look she turned on the man, the sudden blaze of fury in her eyes at having been interrupted. Almost it seemed as if she would strike at the smooth features, then the hand she had lifted quivered a moment and lowered.

As it dropped to her side Kennedy said, "Yes, an aircar. We were crossing the preserve when something happened to throw us out of control. The vehicle crashed and we are lucky to be alive."

"And your companions? The pilot?"

"Dead."

"An unfortunate occurrence," said Royce blandly. "You see, my dear, how easily the mystery is explained. It is obvious that the meteor created an atmospheric turbulence, which would have destroyed any aircraft in the vicinity. These men are fortunate to be alive."

"And dressed as they are?"

Royce shrugged. "A whim of their mistress, perhaps, my dear. They cannot be blamed for that."

She turned from him, tense, uneasy, conscious of unfamiliar reactions as she stared at Kennedy. Royce had been too glib, too fast with his interference, almost as if he were giving signals, certainly a guide. Was he somehow involved with the pair?

And Kennedy disturbed her. She felt herself wishing that he was the one who stood at her side, that he was the consort. Foolishness, probably induced by the drugs she had taken in the wine, but now, for the first time, she felt that she could appreciate the women who were the target of whispered insinuations. Such a man could easily subvert a particular type of woman to his will. Not herself, of course, but—

She said flatly, "You are clever, Royce, perhaps a little too clever, but there are still questions to be answered. From where did they come? To where were they going? From what quadrant do they originate? I think that perhaps the Wardens will be able to persuade them to speak."

With whips and fire and charred finger-ends, Kennedy thought. He tensed as they edged closer, their eyes wide with sadistic anticipation. They were armed with knives and clumsy pistols looking like primitive muzzle-loaders, though there was no sign of an external firing device. Probably some form of shotgun, able to blast a hail of missiles from the snouting barrels. A short-range weapon, easily carried and of more use in the forest than a rifle.

One was closer than the others, his hand extended as if he couldn't wait, loose lips wet with saliva.

He would be the first, Kennedy decided grimly. The edge of his stiffened hand against the neck and then, as he fell, a leap toward the woman, the needler at her throat. The weapon would frighten her—if nothing else they would at least gain time.

Luden groaned.

He lifted one hand to his head and slumped a little, making an obvious effort to maintain his balance and, as obviously, failing. Kennedy caught him as he fell.

"My companion is hurt," he snapped. "He needs rest and attention. Where can I take him?"

The crack of his voice turned the question into a command. Natalie found herself turning, pointing to a small tent beside the pavilion. Royce's tent, but she didn't think of that or the subconscious motivation behind the gesture.

"In there. I shall send you medical aid."

The woman who arrived was small, fussy, making discordant sounds as she examined Luden's slight figure, probing into the mass of his hair.

"Men!" she commented. "When will you weak, silly creatures ever learn? An obvious concussion and you had to make him walk for miles in the hot sun. Well, there it is. Give him rest and some warm liquids. Nothing solid for at least twenty-four hours."

Straight-faced, Kennedy said, "Is the skull fractured, Doctor?"

"I'm not a doctor, just a medical aide, but no, I don't think there is any serious damage. Just do as I say and he will be all right."

Luden sat upright as she left. Sourly he said, "If that woman is a medical aide, then God help the sick in this world. Any first-term medical student would have known that I hadn't a concussion. She didn't even examine my eyes."

"She didn't need to, Jarl. You put on a very convincing performance."

"But a necessary one, Cap. They were about to jump us." Luden looked around the tent. It was bare of luxury, almost spartan in its furnishings. A row of books stood on a low stand fitted with drawers. A chest held clothing, a table carried glasses and a bottle of wine. "Well, at least we have made contact, though I confess that I can't see how it is going to help us. In a sense we are prisoners."

Kennedy crossed to the books, lifted one, riffled through the pages.

"What do you make of it, Jarl?"

"This society?" Luden pursed his lips. "As yet we have little evidence on which to base a firm conclusion, yet some things are clear. I think it logical to assume that we are in a matriarchal culture—it was obvious that the woman was dominant. Also we can gather there are various zones of power. North America, North China, South Africa. The quadrants she spoke of must be confined to either hemisphere, which, if their division follows a logical pattern, would give eight sectors. If they are of equal status there would be rivalry, if not outright hostility. Such a state of affairs would account for the woman's suspicions."

"And the orbiting forts?"

"I don't know, Cap. As yet we have no evidence. The result of mutual distrust, perhaps, or a paranoic fear of invasion." Luden frowned, pursing his thin lips. "What we need is access to a library. There is too much about this world we do not know."

Essentials: A library in order to orient themselves. The essential crystal of zirnalite. Information and equipment to destroy the torus threatening Earth. And they were stuck, semi-prisoners in a hunting camp.

Dropping the book, Kennedy crossed the tent to stand at the flap. It was drawn, but through a gap he could see the camp outside, the pavilion, the aircar around which drab figures worked at their endless polishing.

"Tonight, Jarl," he said quietly. "When it is dark and the camp asleep. We'll take that aircar and be on our way."

"To a city, Cap." Luden nodded his agreement. "Certainly we can do nothing constructive here. But we'll need maps."

"They might be in the cabinet."

"And if not?"

Kennedy turned, his face hard. "If not, Jarl, then we'll take someone with us to show the way."

SILVERBERG

threatened; had not asked. She saw the expression of surprise and rage; no attempt to mask his contempt.

"Did you think I hadn't noticed? What are they to you?"

CHAPTER SEVEN

Royce was uneasy. It had been obvious all through the meal and now, watching him from where she sat at the table, Natalie could almost feel his emotional turmoil, as if it were invisible hands caressing her skin, ants running over exposed nerves. It irritated her, added to her own confusion, so that she finished the wine in a single gulp.

"More, my dear?"

"No." It had been a fresh bottle, untainted with medicines, the cork drawn before her watchful eye. The responsiblity should never have been hers, but who else could she wholly trust? "Something is bothering you, Royce. What is it?"

"Nothing, my dear."

"You're lying. I always know when you lie. Perhaps we have been together too long?" She saw the jerk of muscles at the edge of his jaw, sensed his sudden fear. Cruelly she added, "You have a good brain. Maybe it could be used."

"No!" This time he made no attempt to hide his terror. "No, Natalie! You promised!"

"Only to feed you, house you, tend you when you are ill. Or have you tended," she corrected. "So far I have carrried out my duties; have you yours?"

"As far as—"

"You have been permitted, true." She acknowledged the fact with a slight inclination of her head. "But I need more from a consort than temporary passion. I require truth. What is bothering you?"

"Those men."

"For whom you so conveniently provided answers to

questions I had not asked." She saw the expression on his face and made no attempt to mask her contempt. "Did you think I hadn't noticed? What are they to you?"

"Nothing! I swear it!"

"Then why defend them?" She shook her head, not waiting for an answer, annoyed at herself for having threatened him. That was a sure proof of her inward disturbance. No one as close as he was should ever be threatened. Disposed of, yes, but never driven to a point where, maybe, desperation would cause him to become a threat in turn. "Never mind, Royce. Attend me."

Outside it was dark with early night, the stars a glimmering curtain touched with a crescent moon. She looked at it for a moment, Tycho was still in shadow, the Mare Fecundus an irregular blob. Unknown to herself her hand fell to rest on the flatness of her stomach. The stomach had always been flat, and would never swell to the pulse of inward life.

From behind her, his voice a whisper, Royce said, "Natalie. Those two men. I had to interfere in order to give you time to think. And others were listening. I had to put words in their mouths. If I hadn't they would have said too much."

Remembering Kennedy she doubted it. "Well?"

"The thing which crashed. It wasn't a meteor, no matter what Aerial Command said. It couldn't have been. I know you laugh at my calculations, but mathematics can't be ignored. It wasn't a meteor, Natalie. It had to be a ship."

Tightly she said, as he paused, "Go on."

"A ship, Natalie. And those two men must have come from it. You saw how they were dressed. Even the way they spoke, I mean the way they looked at you as if—" He broke off as if afraid to put it into words.

She did it for him. "As if they were equals? Yes, Royce, I noticed."

She had noticed and had done nothing about it. Why not? Had it been the effects of the wine with its medication? Or had it been that, subconsciously, she had recognized the fact that there had been nothing she could have done? Humbleness was not a part of their character and never would be. They, Kennedy certainly, might accept her as an equal but never as a superior.

Why did she keep thinking of Kennedy?

"They must have jumped out before it crashed," Royce continued. "Those men, I mean. They could have had parachutes or something and abandoned the vessel when they were certain it was out of control." His voice broke, became entreating. "Natalie, about what you said, you would never—"

"Don't worry, Royce. Your brain will die in your body." She would probably keep that promise; now she had more to think about than the calming of his mind.

Aerial Command had been positive that the object had been a meteor and now, oddly, it appeared they could have been wrong and that Royce had been right. The appearance of the strangers had altered her previous conviction. Had Aerial Command lied?

It was possible, perhaps a cover-up for their failure to destroy the vessel. No one would question them. But from where had it come, and why?

Luck, she thought. Her position on the Council was weaker now than it had been for years. If she could obtain clear evidence of conspiracy, perhaps, or at the least inefficiency, she would have a weapon with which to regain power.

Excitement accelerated the beat of her heart as she turned and looked toward the tent in which the men were contained. Guards stood before and around it, Wardens, invisible in the shadows but ever alert. Two of her own guards also, trusted women dedicated to her House.

"My lady!" One saluted as she came close. "They seem to be asleep. There was some talking but in such a low tone that I could make out nothing."

"Have they been fed?"

"Standard fare, my lady. One portion. As your medical aide instructed."

Natalie nodded. Chariam was a good woman despite certain rumors. A little rough at times, perhaps, but that was no crime. And who could believe all that was whispered?

"You intend to enter, my lady?"

"Yes."

"Is it your wish that I accompany you?"

"No, but stand by in case I call." As she stepped toward the flap of the tent Royce, doglike, ran after her.

"Natalie. Please, may I come with you?"

She heard the creak of leather as Chariam stiffened, but the amazon was too hard. Her unspoken disapproval worked to the consort's advantage.

"You may, but be discreet. We are here to learn, not to fill their mouths with words."

A lantern stood on a low table, brought by the porters who had delivered the meal. Kennedy sat in its light, reading, Luden at his side. They rose as she entered.

"My lady." Kennedy met her eyes. He added, "This is a pleasure."

Smooth, she thought, and so self-confident. About him there was no aura of fear. He stood as if he had expected her, almost as if he were glad that she had come.

To Luden she said, "You may sit." Glancing at the books, she continued, "I see that you have been keeping yourselves occupied, but surely a man with a concussion should not read?"

"My friend has remarkable powers of recovery," said Kennedy. "And the aid you supplied was very efficient."

"Elga is a fool, but she is the best available. Did you find the books of interest?"

There were mathematical works, a treatise on conservation, two volumes of poetry, a historical romance based in the time of Augustus, another dealing with the campaign of Boadicea, both the histories written from a woman's point of view. They had taught little. There had been no maps.

"Very interesting," said Kennedy. "Yours?"

"His." Her head jerked to where Royce stood beside the flap. "You are in his tent."

"Thank you." Kennedy looked directly at the man. "You have been most kind."

"We did not come here to exchange compliments," she said harshly. "First let me make it clear that I know you for the liars you are. There is no House of Fren and there is no Selene Var. Persist in that stupid pretense and you will regret it. Do I make myself plain?"

"Very plain," said Kennedy. His face was a mask to hide his racing thoughts. It was impossible for her to know every House and every person of importance in this world, yet she could have had reference books to yield the information. Should he continue the bluff or try another? Royce gave him the clue.

"The ship," he said. "We know you must have come from the ship that crashed."

"Royce!"

"You are right," Kennedy admitted quickly. "My lady, allow me to congratulate you on the intelligence of your consort. There was a ship and we were in it. We came from, well, somewhere."

"From space?"

"Yes."

So Aerial Command had lied, their defensive ring had been broken, and she owned the living proof of their inefficiency. Faced with it Teri Kramer would have no choice other than to resign or back her in the Council. And the woman would never resign.

Natalie drew in her breath, conscious of the racing of her heart, the euphoria which threatened to overwhelm her.

Royce said shrewdly, "But from where in space? And why didn't you use the open channel?"

Kennedy hesitated, a man blindfolded in a dark cellar, cautiously groping his way, knowing that one false move would spell destruction. Yet the chance had to be taken. If the woman could be won over it would save precious time.

"Jarl, explain."

Luden cleared his throat. "Madam, please give me your attention. As you have spaceflight you must have a knowledge of astronomy and, I take it, observatories. If your people will turn their instruments toward the constellation of Bootes they will see, at a point roughly midway between the stars Seginus and Nekkar, an orange torus. By this time it will be approaching the orbit of Neptune. If you plot its path you will discover that it will intersect the orbit of Earth." He added, "The time of intersection will coincide with the presence of the planet. As an intelligent person you can realize the consequences."

She said, "I warned you of the result of lying. Must I call the guards to put you to the torture?"

"Please, Natalie." Royce, at least, had been impressed by Luden's calm delivery. "They could be telling the truth."

"Nonsense!"

"But—"

"Be silent!" Natalie fought to master her rage. In the game she was playing anger could have no part, but it was hard to remain calm. "First the lie about your House and your mistress and now this stupid fabrication. I will give you one, final chance to tell the truth. You came from space, that I will accept, but from where? Luna? Mars?"

"Neither."

"From where then?"

"Through the torus."

"You lie!"

"We came through the torus," Kennedy repeated flatly. "It threatens our world as well as your own. We came to find a means of closing it. A fort tried to destroy us. A fort controlled by a living brain." He saw

Royce recoil, a sick look in his eyes. "We killed it. We gave it peace."

"No!" The woman's anger dissolved to be replaced by a desperate incredulity. "No. You couldn't have. The Zeglar would never have permitted it."

"The Zeglar?"

"Don't add one lie to another," she snapped. "The Zeglar are the Guardians of Earth as you must well know. They protect us. If, somehow, you have destroyed one of their forts they will know it. And you will pay!"

Luden said, "Tell us about the Zeglar."

"Are you both fools?" Natalie stared from one to the other. "Can even men be so ignorant? Or do you take me to be even a bigger fool to believe your tissue of lies?"

"A fool, yes." Kennedy's voice was the crack of a whip. "But worse than that. You are a stupid female who refuses to even consider that she could be wrong. The torus exists—you can check—and it threatens this world. That can be checked also. Damn it, woman, we are telling you the truth!"

She recoiled as if he had slapped her in the face, unable to believe that she had been insulted so grossly, that any man would dare to talk as he had done.

"Chariam!"

Luden fired as the amazon stepped into the tent, the dart thudding into her cheek, her thickset, heavy body falling with a creak of leather, the rattle of accouterments. As Natalie opened her mouth to scream Kennedy stepped forward, his own needler in hand, the snout pressing against her throat.

"No noise, my lady," he said grimly. "Jarl?"

Luden was at the flap of the tent. "No one coming, Cap, but there are guards waiting beyond earshot."

"The Wardens." Royce gulped, his eyes wide. "Please don't shoot her."

"I'll kill her if I have to." Kennedy saw no point in explaining that the darts were harmless. "You too unless you cooperate. There are clothes in that chest; get them. And money if you have it. Are there any maps?"

"Only of this area. They are in the pavilion."

"Leave them." Kennedy looked at the woman. She stood close, rigid, stunned by the savage turn of events. "Listen, my lady, we are going to leave here and you will help us to do it. You and your consort both. Do you understand?"

She had been right about his mouth, now it was cruel, a match for the eyes which blazed with determination. And for the first time in her life she was afraid of a man, knowing that her sex and rank were now no protection. It didn't help to know she had been the worst kind of fool. They should have been searched— but who would have thought men would have dared so much?

"I will ask you once more," said Kennedy. His voice matched the eyes, the mouth, the tones of a man who would brook no disobedience. "Do you understand that unless you cooperate fully you will regret it?"

She nodded, swallowing, finding it hard to talk as her throat was so dry. "What do you intend to do?"

"You have an aircar; we shall use it. Jarl?"

"Ready, Cap." Luden had changed, his thin figure draped in dull brown, a twin to the insignia Royce wore on his breast. "I'll stand guard while you get ready."

As he changed Royce asked, a little unsteadily, "Who are you? Freemen?"

"We are free, yes, and we are men, but not in the way you mean. On our world men do not permit themselves to be treated like dogs."

"You are fortunate."

"Not fortunate; sane. No one respects a doormat, a woman least of all. You should remember that." Kennedy moved to the flap, the brown he wore straining at back and shoulders. Dim shapes stood against the stars, one of them a woman who came close.

"My lady?"

"Answer her!" Luden lifted the muzzle of the needler so that she could see the narrow orifice. "Quickly!"

"It is all right," called Natalie. "Return to your station."

Kennedy said, "Royce, can you pilot the aircar? Good. This is what we shall do. All of us together will leave the tent and head toward it. Can you give orders? Will you be obeyed?" He sensed the other's indecision, his reluctance to admit his inferiority. "Never mind. The woman can do it. Tell her."

"There is no need," she said coldly. "I have heard."

"And you will obey." Kennedy replaced Luden at her side. "Any trouble and I fire. Watch the man, Jarl. Ready? Then let's go."

To Natalie it was a strange journey. Walking, with Kennedy close to her side, knowing that he would do exactly as he had threatened, anger struggled against a less familiar emotion. The insult was unpardonable, of course, but even so there was something about his nearness, the radiated strength of him, which appealed to something deeply buried within her primeval subconscious.

In early times such a man had been indispensable to the perpetuation of the race. A warrior to guard and protect his women and their young. A hunter to provide essential food. A tower of strength against the terrifying perils of the unknown. That situation had now long vanished, and yet something of that early need still remained.

If Royce had been like Kennedy would she have so brutally rejected his effort to be more to her than what he was?

Guards rose before the little party, to fall back at her command. With a strange detachment she saw Royce enter the aircar, Luden following, and felt Kennedy's pressure urging her into the compartment. It was the first time he had actually touched her and his hand, like his face, was strong.

Then they were aloft, with the engine humming and the camp falling away below.

At the controls Royce said, "Where shall I take you?"

"To a city. A large one." Luden looked at the map unreeling on the panel, the point of light which gave their position. "Somewhere close."

"Bymark is the nearest." Royce altered course a little. "It is the capital of this sector. We live there."

"Cap?"

"It will do, Jarl." A flight into danger, perhaps, but it couldn't be helped, Kennedy thought. At least Royce would know his way, and the aircar would be familiar to any watchful guards. To the woman he said, "Think over what we have told you. Get your technicians to check the torus. If it is to be closed we need all the help we can get."

"Help for liars and thieves?" Her tone was chilling. "Killers also? I think not."

"Listen," said Kennedy harshly. "You belong to the Council and I assume that means you have some sense. Forget your hurt pride. Remember that those you rule depend on you. If nothing else check on what you have been told. Damn it, woman! The fate of this world depends on it!"

The raw sincerity in his voice was unmistakable, not the whine of a coward. And yet he was nothing but a man.

She said coldly, "This farce has continued long enough. You will put down your weapons and obey my commands. Shortly we shall be challenged by a patrol. I shall order them to restrain this aircar. You will be questioned and the truth determined."

Kennedy shot her.

Royce turned at the small sound of the needler, the slap as the dart buried itself into the flesh of her shoulder. Supporting the limp figure, Kennedy said quickly, "She isn't dead, just unconscious. I had to do it."

"Why?"

Kennedy had sensed hysteria in her voice, the crumbling of restraint as warring emotions caused an inner conflict. She had made a threat and he knew she would have carried it out.

"You heard her," Kennedy said grimly. "If we are challenged can you get us past the patrol?"

"Yes."

"Are you certain? If not, land and we'll proceed on foot."

"That wouldn't be wise." Royce turned, not looking at them as he busied himself with the controls. "I'll get you to the city."

CHAPTER EIGHT

It was big, sprawling, sections of housing interspersed with industries, shops and manufacturing plants mixed with offices. And it held slums.

From the window of a sleazy hotel Kennedy looked at the morning light. For three days now they had roved the city. The money taken from Royce had been quickly dissipated, but more was obtained by the sale of gems they had carried from the *Mordain*. In those three days they had learned the mores, rules, and politics of a new world.

Luden sighed as he closed the last of a heap of books.

"As far as I can determine, Cap, the divergence from our own history took place shortly after the Debacle. More proof if we needed it that we are on an alternate world to our own. In our own history we managed to survive and went on to establish the *Pax Terra*. Here, apparently, there were complications."

Militant feminists had risen to spread fresh havoc among the ruins. In the war the male population, already depleted by the conflict, had fallen victim to a plague which induced early death and monstrous change. The virus attacked the prostate and destroyed essential male hormones. It was a bad time during which had come a second dark age, when vast areas of technology were lost and forgotten, the population reduced to a fragment of what it had once been, the race struggling to survive against crushing odds.

And Luden had called it a complication!

"The development of parthenogenesis was of prime importance," he continued in his thin, dry tones, "and was extremely successful, but, of course, could only perpetuate the females of the species. If it hadn't been for a few males who were immune to the plague this would be now a literal world of women. However, the masculine semen was used, despite violent opposition from the more extreme of the militants, to provide artificial insemination of a number of low-echelon females. They became, in effect, brood mares and were despised because of it."

"Nice," Kennedy said dryly. He wondered what it had been like to be a potent male during that period. The literature gave the impression that, far from being valued and pampered members of the community, they had been treated like stud bulls, imprisoned, restrained, used only to provide seed. "At least a few of them had sense, even though parthenogenesis was so successful. They recognized the need to maintain the available gene pool."

"Exactly, Cap. They realized the dead end they were entering and did something about it. But not without opposition. The pro-path and the pro-seed had a war in which a compromise was reached. Fertilized ova were placed in artificial wombs to reach maturity. Women were therefore freed of what they termed the tyranny of pregnancy and yet the race could still survive."

Rising, Luden joined Kennedy at the window. Both men now wore dull gray denims devoid of any insignia.

"A strange society, Cap," he mused. "A matriarchy based on a feudal system of estates and Houses. Men are considered to be inferior and are used only to perform menial tasks. Consorts, or what we would call husbands, have no legal rights and can be dismissed at any time. The children of such unions take the name of their mother. After birth they are reared in state nurseries and taught according to their sex. Girls are given a good education, boys, unless very high in the social scale, are given only the basics, and even then the extra education is only concerned with cultural mores."

Kennedy said thoughtfully, "Royce was interested in mathematics, his books showed us that."

"A whim, Cap, a hobby to any woman who knew of it. They would never take him seriously."

A pity, the man would have been an ally. They had left him unconscious beside Natalie, needled as she had been, lying in the aircar after he had landed it close to town. It was an essential precaution, as Kennedy had explained and Royce had accepted.

A brave man in his way, Royce had only Kennedy's word that the darts were harmless. He had helped them on the way to the city with information and the promise of more aid if he could give it. Empty words, perhaps, but Kennedy didn't think so.

And he had told them of the Zeglar.

Kennedy's lips thinned as he remembered the fort and the living brain it had contained.

The Zeglar were alien. The race had come a century ago from the stars, offering technological aid and protection—for a price.

The price was human, living brains.

Male brains, of course; the women would permit no other. The brains were the essential elements of the cyborg computer devices. They were the compact, highly efficient control units of the forts, the orbiting vessels, and the spacecraft which plied the system.

"The Zeglar!" Kennedy looked down at his hands. They were closed into fists, the knuckles white. "The Earth enslaved, Jarl. It doesn't seem possible."

"On our world, no, Cap," Luden admitted. "But we were never contacted by an alien race. By the time we reached the stars and contacted other cultures our defenses were secure. Here it was different. The culture had stagnated, an almost inevitable result of feminine rule. Women are, by nature, conservative. Compared to men they are mature, lacking the permanent adolescence which leads to the desire for adventure and exploration. And space-flight, initially, offers nothing but a tremendous expense with no immediate reward. And they had trouble after the Debacle that we managed to avoid."

That trouble had cost them hard-learned sciences,

causing them to look inward instead of outward, directing all their energies in one narrow channel.

And the Zeglar had come with gifts, knowledge of how to make fertilizers from air, how to drill and find residual resources, how to construct computers after a certain pattern. Even knowledge of spaceflight, which had opened up other worlds.

Toys with which they had bought a planet.

Bought it and enslaved it.

The forts, supposedly for defense, were a prison to confine the aliens' prize. Here was a source of easily acquired raw material for alien constructs, willingly given, unable to resist once totally dominated. And that domination would come, Kennedy was certain of it.

"The aliens have cheated, Cap," said Luden. "Nowhere in the books can I find mention of atomic power. And they seem to know nothing of hydrive. Yet the Zeglar must have a means of faster-than-light travel. It would be essential if they were to conduct any form of commerce with their own worlds."

"To them we are savages taking the trade goods they offer for what we can supply. It is natural they would cheat."

"True, Cap, but we cannot get involved. Our own problems are serious enough. Penza has repaired the *Mordain* as far as he is able without the crystal of zirnalite. We must find one—a problem. We must get it to the ship—another. And then we must search for some way to close the torus—a third." Luden lifted his thin shoulders in a shrug. "I see no way in which we can defeat the Zeglar."

"Yet we have to use them, Jarl," Kennedy said flatly. "Or their products. This world has nothing to offer in the way of science and new technologies other than that supplied by the Zeglar. The green energy which wrecked the *Mordain* is something new."

"An application of electronic stress to the graviton structure," admitted Luden. "At least that is what it seemed to be. If we could discharge it in quantity against the torus, perhaps—" He broke off, irritable as he shook his head. "Speculation will not help us, Cap. We need concrete proof. And that means a laboratory, test equipment, facilities we do not have."

"No, Jarl, but maybe we can get them. First we have to repair the *Mordain*." Kennedy looked through the window at the mass of the sprawling city. "Zirnalite," he said. "Let's go and find some."

The owner of the hotel stepped out from where he had been lurking in his dingy office as they reached the bottom of the stairs. He was a small, greasy man, balding, dressed in dull olive. His eyes were bloodshot and his denims were stained with cheap wine.

"You going out?"

"Yes,"' said Kennedy.

"Coming back?"

"We've paid for the week. We'll be back. Why the questions?"

"Nothing, just checking. I've a right to ask, haven't I?" Scowling, the man scratched at his chin, then said abruptly, "If you're looking for work I hear they're taking on sweepers at the Arnet-Lemurge. It's three blocks down and one to the left. You want work?"

Kennedy nodded.

"Then try them. If it's a bust I might have something else. You'll be back?"

"Yes," said Kennedy. "We'll be back."

He led the way down the street as if going to the plant, passing it and the thin line of men waiting for a job. As they fell behind he said, "We'd best move, Jarl. They could be getting close."

"That man certainly acted oddly, Cap." Luden looked back then to one side. No one was following and no one was walking in their direction. "Probably a police spy but a very amateur one. Or he could even have been giving us a warning. In any case it would be unwise to return. Which alternative?"

"The third." Kennedy had marked out several small hotels in various areas of the city where they could rendezvous if separated. "Now let us see if we can get some zirnalite."

To try small jewelers would be a waste of time; already he had decided that the most likely place would be at the industrial complex of Henge-Cormile Lan, a firm specializing in synthetics.

The receptionist, a middle-aged woman of low-echelon, stared coldly at their gray clothes, then thawed a little at Kennedy's smile.

"Zirnalite?" She frowned. "No, I'm sure we don't produce it. In fact I've never heard of it. Are you sure you have the right name?"

"Perhaps not," Kennedy smiled. "In fact I'm not even sure that someone isn't having a joke at our expense. But we have to try. A job depends on it." He stared . . . enviously at the insignia on her tunic, and tried to appeal to her sympathy for him as a fellow underling. "I'm sure you understand, my lady. Sometimes things can be hard."

The woman said, "Well, I'm not sure, but can you describe it?"

Luden cleared his throat. "A crystal of pure isometric proportions approximately one inch long with an atomic weight of 186.3, atomic number 107, valency zero. Resistance to a current of fifteen amps is 0.0013 ohms. Refractive index—" He broke off, aware of her expression. "Am I making sense, my lady?"

"Indeed you are." Her amazement was genuine. "But how you, a man, and—" She frowned at his clothing. "Who asked you to obtain this?"

"The Lady Cilla Umyer," Kennedy said smoothly. "Of the House of Charlet." The name and House were genuine, culled from his studies. "Naturally we did not see her in person; the instructions came from a member of her retinue."

"A woman?"

"A man, my lady."

"There's nothing so bitchy as a snotty male," she said with vigor. "You're right; he was having fun at your expense. I suppose he told you that you could have work if you delivered the crystal?"

Kennedy nodded, looking abashed. "Are you saying there is no such thing, my lady?"

"There is, but you had the name wrong. We call it zimaze-x." She pointed to a showcase hanging against a wall. Behind thick glass rested a row of polished crystals, samples set out for display. "There, the upper row, the third from the right. Exactly as you described it to within a fraction. The cost is fifteen thousand nudols."

A lot of money, more than they had or could hope to get. Kennedy turned, studying the reception chamber, noting the doors, the windows, the general area.

Politely he said, "Thank you for your kindness, my lady. Obviously someone is having a joke. I apologize for any inconvenience we may have caused."

She sighed as he left, remembering his smile, his radiated charm, mentally comparing him to her consort and half-regretting that she hadn't yielded to temptation. Still, it wouldn't have done. Low though her echelon was, it and her position demanded responsibility and, after all, he had worn gray. A pity.

Outside in the street, Luden said urgently, "The crystal, Cap. It was exactly what we need. Tonight?"

"Yes, Jarl. We'll steal it after dark."

They killed the afternoon in a cinema, cramped in narrow seats and watching adventures in which the females were always strong, the men always dutifully obedient. Kennedy would have found the old-fashioned pastime amusing in other circumstances. At night they returned to the showroom of Henge-Cormile Lan. The building was dark, only a soft light illuminating the area beyond the door, little sparkles coming from the crystals assembled in the case.

Kennedy stooped, a sliver of metal in his hand as he picked at the lock. As footsteps came close along the sidewalk, he suddenly doubled over and groaned loudly, as if in pain.

"Help!" Luden's voice held anxiety. "Please help me. My friend is ill.'"

The footsteps slowed, halted, moved on as a

woman's voice snapped, "Pay no attention, Marge. The man is probably drunk. It's time the patrols cleared the streets of such scum."

The lock clicked open as she finished speaking and passed by.

Kennedy straightened.

"Jarl?"

"Clear so far, Cap."

Standing in clear view of the street, the area illuminated, the case protected by thick glass, only speed could be of use.

Kennedy thrust open the door, snatched up a chair and slammed it against the case with the full force of back and shoulders. The metal chair bent and cracks appeared on the glass. Another blow splintered it.

Throwing aside the chair, Kennedy cleared the frame, snatched the essential crystal, and, turning, threw it toward Luden. He caught it, tucked it into a pocket, and immediately ran away. Taking time only to snatch other crystals Kennedy followed him, turning in the opposite direction down the street.

He heard the harsh note of a siren, and halted as cars came humming down the street. For a second he stood beneath a standard, clear in the cone of light, then ran, stooped, throwing a crystal behind him as he raced toward the mouth of an alley.

After him came the police.

They were fast, trained women, tall and lithe, young and with muscles like steel. Kennedy heard a shouted command and dodged aside as a pistol roared, chips of stone spraying from the wall close to a point where he had stood. Again he ran, leading the police away from Luden and the precious crystal, following a path he had mapped earlier in the day.

The street was filled with wide-eyed pedestrians, and traffic squealed to a halt as he wove between the cars. A wailing siren and more police were ahead, their weapons lifted and ready to fire.

He beat them to it, the needler spraying darts, and uniform shapes fell as he ran toward them, jumping over the slumped bodies, throwing aside more of the crystals as he ran, sure proof that he was the thief and that they chased the true quarry.

He came to a lane, swarmed over a high bordering wall, and landed on a small narrow street. A truck was lumbering down the street, a heavy transport laden with bales, the load lashed with thick ropes. Kennedy raced toward it, fingers reaching for the bindings, gripping them as the speed of the vehicle jerked the ground from beneath his feet. For a moment he swung and then, like a cat, climbed to the top of the load and lay prone as the truck ground through the night.

As it left the city he lifted his arm, and lips close to the commmunicator, said, "Penza?"

"No, Cap, it's Veem. Are you all right?"

"Yes. Jarl?"

"He's safe, Cap," said Chemile. "You drew away the pursuit. He's waiting as arranged."

A deeper voice as Saratov joined the conversation.

"You're taking too many chances, Cap. Be careful."

"How long will it take you to fit the crystal, Penza?"

"Not long. I can cut it if I have to." An anxious note came into the giant's voice. "'But how are you going to get it here?"

"That's why I'm calling. Tell Jarl to wait until dawn, no longer. If I haven't joined him by then he's to act as best as he sees fit."

"And you, Cap?"

"I'm going to try to get some help."

Kennedy looked up as rain spattered on his hand. The sky was dark, heavy with cloud, detail impossible to see beyond the glare of the vehicle's headlights. A bad night to be out in strange terrain and the truck was carrying him farther from the city each second. He could not afford to wait for it to slow down.

Moving to the rear of the load he slipped down the ropes, and swinging his feet before him, released his hold. The vehicle was traveling fast, the ground slammed beneath his feet, jerking them from beneath him, causing him to fall, rolling in trained reflex over the concrete toward the side of the road, the ditch which edged it.

The ditch and the gnarled root of a tree against which he struck with stunning force.

CHAPTER NINE

All day the air had been heavy and at midnight the weather broke with rolling thunder echoing from the horizon, lightning searing the air like jagged darts misted with rain. That storm was accompanied by its counterpart in the Council Chamber, a fitting match for the turmoil of emotions that ruled.

Tiredly Natalie Toluca rested her head in her hands, elbows on the polished wood of the table, the scatter of papers between them a visible symbol of her defeat.

Five ballots, and she had lost them all. The Hitachi-Olmouta had sunk their claws deep and the prize they had won would be paid in blood. Tana Golchika had managed to maneuver her favorites into high positions and, as she had suspected, the vote on the Melford-Phrindah amalgamation, retaken at her insistence, had swept the board in their favor.

She had been outgunned, outvoted, outmaneuvered all along the line. Never had her standing in Council been so low.

She sighed, feeling the constriction of her chest, the nagging pain at her heart, the physical results of the tension that consumed her. Drugs would ease it but their tranquilizing effect would dull the sharp edge of her mind and here, among these she-wolves, she dared not risk giving them any further advantage.

"My dear, you look all in. Perhaps you should leave now and get some rest. I'm sure the rest of the business can be managed without the benefit of your opinions."

Natalie stirred at the sound of the hatefully familiar voice. Teri Kramer, resplendent in the uniform she always wore, a thin, acid smile on her hard, cold face, stood at her side.

"A pity that you lost so often, but well, my dear, these things happen. We all grow old. I'm sure that you would feel better after a hot bath, some massage, and a good sleep. From what I am told such treatment can work wonders."

Natalie straightened in her chair, conscious of watching eyes, the others of the Council enjoying her discomfiture.

Coldly she said, "So I am given to understand, Teri. Perhaps you should try it."

"I, my dear?" Thin brows rose over the deep-set eyes. "Surely I have displayed no need of such attention. After all, I am not under medical care."

The bitch! Twisting the knife in the wound and adding to the insult. Or perhaps it was the first step in a contrived plan. Caution halted Natalie's instinctive rejoinder. A public quarrel now would only serve to provide her enemies with ammunition. First the hint that she was too weak and ill to be fit for office, then the subtle pressure for her to resign followed by outright hostility and contrived impeachment.

She had seen it all happen before, had even arranged it. Diane Kent, who had left quietly. Guirda Han, who had been ready to fight and who had been found dead before the final humiliation could be delivered.

Had her secret been used against her? Had the verdict been genuine; that she had actually taken her own life and had not been the victim of an asssassin?

Dropping into a chair beside her, Teri Kramer said softly, "Let us understand each other, Natalie. I will not pretend that we are friends, but I bear you no hate. I would not like to see you publicly shamed and humiliated. You are ill, that is common knowledge, and it would be natural for you to find the burden of your duties too heavy to bear."

Natalie stiffened as the soft voice fell silent. It was coming, but sooner than she had expected.

"So?"

"A resignation would be in order, don't you think? We would all understand. And I think you will admit it is only common sense to accept the inevitable gracefully. As you say, your credit with the Council is low. No one voted with you on any of the issues. And, really, my dear, you have no choice but to resign."

"There is always a choice, Teri."

"True," admitted the other woman. "But think of the alternative. Guirda Han was a very foolish woman. She was not only indiscreet but willful to a fault. Your consort—"

"Royce?"

"—is the living proof of her stupidity. Surely you have heard the rumors?"

Natalie felt her throat go dry, her stomach contracting at the chasm she faced. Water stood on the table and she sipped a little, fighting for self-control.

"Royce is Guirda's natural-born son," whispered Teri, a thin undertone of malice in her voice. "She bore him and carried him to term. He was raised in secrecy on her estate at Formelaque and introduced into society only when old enough to have learned to guard his tongue. Naturally she wanted to safeguard him with a strong attachment. At the time you seemed to be the best."

It happened. Women who defied all common sense and convention, insisting on bearing their own young. Usually they were of the lower-echelons, suffering shame and ignominy, their children low-caste forever. But Guirda Han?

Natalie remembered her, a tall, strong woman with a soft mouth and warm eyes, hips and breasts larger than current fashion dictated. An earthy creature, she had thought, but with a deep and gentle compassion. And she had chosen to die in order to save her son from shame, to protect the position she had worked so hard to gain, the safety she had imagined would always be his.

"Of course, my dear, you are not to blame," continued Teri Kramer. "But you know how it is. Once the story is out, who will believe that you acted in ignorance? After all, Guirda did help you to reach high office. You did benefit from the association. Now if you were to resign, in a week, say, the secret could remain between us."

But for how long? Women gossiped and were always ready for scandal. And Teri was no friend, as she had admitted. Once Natalie had left the Council the woman would talk. There would be sneers, vile comments, obscene innuendos. The talk would die, of course, but before it did Natalie would be ostracized, stripped of all power and responsibility, derided and shamed.

Society would never forgive her and neither would her House.

Natalie sipped a little more water, feeling calmer now that it was out, and she knew exactly what she had to face.

And attack was always the best defense.

"You have proof of this, Teri?"

The woman smiled, not answering.

No proof then, at least nothing concrete. Guirda would have seen to that. At the best there could be only the testimony of servants and porters, all of whom could be bribed. And yet Guirda had died, weakened perhaps by her own guilty knowledge, and in dying, had removed for all time the one witness who could have proved the allegation.

Again she said, "You have proof, Teri?"

"You are thinking of fighting, Natalie? Believe me it would be a mistake. I have all the evidence I need."

It was another evasion and Natalie could guess why. Things implied needed no displayed proof. Mud, once thrown, could never be wholly washed away. With sudden clarity she realized that her only defense lay in discrediting the woman. To break her so completely that anything she might say afterward would be taken for the spiteful lies of a vengeful mind.

Rising, she said in a loud voice, "I call the Council to order! I wish to move a motion to impeach Teri

Kramer for her failure as Chief of Aerial Command to maintain the security of this planet!"

It was as if she had thrown a bombshell. For a moment they looked at her, a long dragging second in which the roar of nearby thunder sounded frighteningly loud. As the echoes died and faded Teri's voice rasped at her side.

"You fool! What are you doing?"

Helen Estaler repeated the question, then went on: "As the elected head of the Council I must accept all motions proposed, but I fail to see the basis for the move to impeach Teri Kramer. Perhaps, Natalie Toluca, you will explain."

It was a command, Natalie knew. If she refused to explain or if the explanation was unsatisfactory, she was damned.

"During the past week in an area north of this city, at a point close to the mountains of the Oppentock Reserve, an object fell from the sky. Aerial Command stated that it was a meteor which disintegrated on impact. That statement is a lie. The object was not a meteor but a vessel from space. Therefore the basis for my motion is twofold—we have been deluded by an incorrect report, and the fact that the vessel was not destroyed by the forts of Aerial Command is clear proof of the inefficiency of Teri Kràmer, its chief."

"Teri?"

"That an object fell is true," she admitted. "We have never denied it. But to say that it was a ship and not a meteor is ridiculous. I am afraid that Natalie is a little upset at some news she has just received and we must be patient with her. I—and I am sure you of the Council—will be satisfied with a complete retraction."

Helen Estaler frowned, not liking to have words put into her mouth, and Natalie remembered there had been friction between the two women on an earlier occasion.

"I will not retract," Natalie said firmly. "The safety of this planet is paramount and must take precedence over anyone's personal feelings. I realize that Teri is reluctant to admit that her force could be less efficient than she would like; however, the facts remain. A vessel came from space and was not intercepted and destroyed. If one could penetrate our defenses then so could others. I demand a complete investigation."

"Of what?" snapped Teri. "The area was examined and the signs all go to prove that a meteor was responsible. No wreckage was found. If a ship landed, where is it?"

"I did not say that it landed, only that it penetrated our defenses. That, surely, is enough to give us concern. Especially when the fault is compounded with lies. Or are we to believe that Aerial Command cannot tell the difference between a meteor and a vessel?" Her voice was acid, the sarcasm cutting like a knife at Teri's self-possession.

Flushing, Teri snapped, "Are we to listen to the ravings of a desperate woman? I can tell the Council why she has chosen to make this ridiculous accusation. It is a means by which she—"

"Enough!" Helen's gavel thudded against its block. "Teri, control yourself! A serious allegation has been made and must be investigated. Rest assured that if Natalie has lied, she will have cause to regret it. As yet we lack evidence to either substantiate her statement or reject it. But, as she says, the safety of Earth is paramount. Natalie, what proof do you have that it was a vessel and not a meteor?"

She had been dreading the question, but had seen no way to avoid. If only she had managed to confine those two men! If only the police now searching could find them! Their testimony, true or not, would have been sufficient to justify her accusation.

"The proof lies, surely, in the records of Aerial Command. The object must have been spotted and details noted. Photographs, even."

"Of a meteor, yes." Teri relaxed a little, certain of her command of the situation. "An attempt was made to destroy it while it was still in space. The attempt failed, but it must have been either diminished in size or had its mass broken into fragments, most of which would have disintegrated while in transit through the atmosphere. Only the central portion managed to reach the ground with the inevitable result of complete destruction. As I said a search was made and no fragments were found."

An impasse. One woman's word against the other and, as the accuser, Natalie had weakened her case by the absence of proof. A pity, Teri Kramer was already too strong and Natalie's defeat would add to her prestige. And, as things were, her defeat was certain. Teri would provide photographs of a meteor, genuine or not, and who could argue?

Not for the first time Helen Estaler considered that Teri Kramer held too much power.

Helen said flatly, "A deadlock. I am sorry, Natalie, but without proof you have no case. We shall ask for photographs, naturally, but I am certain they will prove Teri's explanation. If you have other evidence?"

Natalie said firmly, "I appeal to the Zeglar!"

It took time to arrange the connection, time in which there was space for thought. The appeal had been a last-ditch hope, yet now that she considered it she wondered why she hadn't thought of it before. An instinctive dislike of the aliens, perhaps; never had she liked what they did, justified as it seemed. Yet, if a vessel had come from space surely they, the Guardians, would know?

The face on the screen was—distasteful. Eyes should not have façets, a nose should be more than a palpitating slit, a mouth something other than a gash lined with rows of small, pointed teeth. And a head should not be crested with spines, ears like holes rimmed with bone, a jaw which looked like a horn.

The voice, too, was disturbing.

"What is it?"

"A matter of prime urgency," said Helen Estaler as head of the Council. "A matter to be settled which falls within your province as Guardians of Earth." She explained it. "Well?"

"There was no vessel."

"What?" Disappointment made Natalie's voice sharp. "Are you certain as to that?"

"There was no ship. If there was we would have destroyed it. Our sworn duty as Guardians of your world would have made it essential. You have nothing to fear. The threat from beyond which we have explained is being kept at bay. The cost, however, is high. I will take advantage of this contact to forewarn you of the necessity to increase the supply of raw material. The next delivery must be the greater by a quarter."

More brains to be turned into machines! Natalie felt the others tense, Helen Estaler's catch of breath. Now the woman would realize what she had done; seduced by the Hitachi-Olmouta the Nord-Am Quadrant would have to meet half of their quota.

But the woman tried. "No! It is too much!"

"Then we must withdraw our protection." The hissing, grating sibilation was cold. "There have been heavy losses in the third decant. Continued, they will make it impossible to maintain our defense. However, the choice is yours."

"We will think about it." Helen swallowed, knowing what the decision would be. "But you are certain that no ship reached us from space?"

"An unauthorized vessel, no."

"Wait!" Natalie pressed forward to the screen, hardly knowing what she did. "One other question. Is there a torus in the constellation of Bootes?"

For a moment the alien made no reply, then said slowly, "There is evidence of a spatial disturbance in that region, yes. It is minor and need cause you no concern."

"Can you close it?"

Again the hesitation. "Our technicians have the matter in hand. There will be no more questions. Do not forget the increased quota. That is all."

A dismissal, a little more abrupt than usual, the arrogance a little less hidden. On the way home Natalie thought about it, preferring to brood over the incident rather than what had followed.

The smiles, the barely veiled hostility, Teri's eyes promising revenge. Only the lateness of the hour had prevented a full session of Council to demand her resignation. That and Helen's sympathy, her dislike of Teri Kramer which had showed itself in her insistence that they defer it until the next session.

A week and it would be all over. Her name and reputation gone. Disowned by her House, shamed and forced to live the rest of her life on a reduced income in some tiny hamlet.

She would be better dead.

Natalie considered it as the aircar landed and servants rushed to usher her into the house. To take a handful of pills, to lie in warm water, to fall asleep and drown. To die as Guirda Han had died, maintaining her reputation to the last.

Irritably she shook her head. Later, perhaps, but there was plenty of time. Now she had other things to consider.

Had the Zeglar lied?

Kennedy had spoken of the torus, and leaning back in the chair in her study, eyes closed, she could again see his face, the hard insistence that stamped mouth and jaw. They had come through a torus, he'd said, and had described exactly where it was to be found. No, Luden, the other one, had done that.

How had they known it was there?

The Zeglar had admitted it existed. Why? Because Terrestrial astronomers could have already discovered it, and had the Zeglar denied it was there they would have shown themselves to be untruthful. Then why should they have lied about the ship if there had been a vessel at all?

To maintain the pretense that they had earth so well guarded that nothing from space could break through their defenses.

Simple. So simple once the truth was known. The

truth that the Zeglar were not wholly what they seemed.

Why hadn't she believed Kennedy? Helped him when she had the chance?

Opening her eyes, she leaned forward and depressed a button on her desk. A quiet voice came from the speaker.

"My lady?"

"Iris, summon Royce. Have him come to me immediately."

One thing at least could be settled. He could not know for certain if he was Guirda's natural son, but he would remember his early years. And, perhaps, she had let something slip in his presence.

Waiting, she remembered. His gentleness, his attempt to help her in her work as if it were something to which he had grown accustomed. His undoubted intelligence and his knowledge of oddities: mathematics, for example, and botany; his deduction that it could not have been a meteor that had landed but a ship. Where had he gained such knowledge?

And other things. The way he had tried to defend her. The way she had woken comfortably cradled in his arms.

And she had threatened him with the loss of his brain.

Not his brain, his body, she mentally corrected; the brain would live on, and she felt something smart her eyes at the thought of it. Royce, the living part of a machine. Royce, who had mixed her wine with medications, who had urged her to rest, who had fretted over her comforts.

Again she touched the button. "Iris, have you located him yet?"

"No, my lady. He is not to be found."

"A message?"

"Not from Royce, my lady, but one from the police. They have found one of the men you ordered them to look for. The old one."

Not Kennedy, then, but Luden would serve. He was

living proof that she had not lied. And one would serve as bait to snare the other.

"Have them bring him here to me immediately," she snapped. "You understand? Immediately!"

She rose, smiling, no longer fatigued. Triumph accelerated the beat of her heart and made her almost giddy with euphoria. With indisputable evidence she would have Teri Kramer at her mercy, the entire Council brought to heel.

Crossing the room, she opened the curtains, the window, and stood looking out into the night. The storm was over, stars shining between masses of scudding cloud. It was almost dawn and would be a wonderful day.

CHAPTER TEN

The woman had a round face, a mass of tangled curls, protruding teeth, and a fuzz of dark hair on her upper lip. Looking at Kennedy, she said, "Hell, you look a mess. What happened? You get hit by a truck?"

"Something like that."

"Some of these drivers don't know how to handle a wheel! A man, I'll bet! Was it a man?"

"Yes," said Kennedy. "I think so. I couldn't see much in the glare of the headlights."

"So he clipped you, eh? Knocked you smack in the ditch. Cracked up your head some by the look of it." She sucked thoughtfully at her teeth. "Well, climb in. I guess I can lift you to town, but we'll have to go the long way 'round."

The seat was hard, the springs nonexistent, but at least it was transport. He leaned back, trying to cushion his aching head. His denims were ruined, stained with dirt and dried blood, more blood caked on the side of his head from a shallow gash received when he'd hit the root of the tree. For an hour he'd lain unconscious, struggling to his feet to be dazzled by the lights of the truck that had stopped.

"I'm making some pickups," said the woman. "Eggs and milk from local farms. You can help me load."

"How long will it take?"

"The trip?" She shrugged. "A couple of hours or so. We'll hit the city around dawn. What's your name?" She frowned as he gave it. "Kennedy? Hell, how about Ken?"

"It'll do."

"I'm Luchia. You tied up?"

"No."

"Reason I ask is because maybe your woman got herself a man to run you down. It happens, and who the hell cares? Or maybe you're a runaway heading for the preserve. They tell me there's lots of Freemen out there. Nuts I call them. Scared of being turned over to the Zeglar. So they lost out, so what? We all have to go sometime." She turned into a narrow lane and halted. "Out and load. The stuff's on a platform."

By their third stop Kennedy had found a pump and washed the blood from his head and hands as the woman impatiently gunned the engine. At the fifth he found clean denims hanging on a line, dull brown with a green insignia, and changed, leaving his own behind.

The woman whistled as she saw him.

"Well, that's better, but how was I to know you'd turn thief? That's bad. I guess I should report it, and maybe I will if you're not nice to me. How about it? You gonna be nice?"

Kennedy shot her in the thigh.

She fell forward over the wheel, her weight triggering the horn, which blased a loud note. From the farmhouse lights shone and a woman's voice, high and shrill, called, "Who's out there? Is that you, Luchia? Luchia?"

The horn died as Kennedy dragged her from the wheel. Thrusting the limp body to the passenger seat, he slipped behind the wheel and sent the truck humming back the way it had come. As he hit the main road he felt the pulse of the attention signal from the communicator on his wrist.

It was Chemile, his voice betraying strain.

"Cap! What happened to you? I've been trying to make contact."

"A little trouble, Veem. Nothing serious. What is it?"

"They've got Jarl, Cap. He managed to open the channel and we heard him taken. They were rough with him, wanting to find you."

"The crystal?"

"I don't know, Cap. He didn't say what he'd done with it, but I think he was delirious or something. It isn't like him to joke, yet when they asked where you were he kept telling them to look under the bed. Crazy, they knew you couldn't be there."

"No," Kennedy said grimly. "But I know what could."

"The crystal?" Chemile drew in his breath. "Of course, a code! Why didn't I think of it! But, Cap, chances are the place will be watched."

"Yes, Veem, I know. Now listen. You might get a visit from a stranger. If you do he'll identify himself with the first two lines of the twelfth verse of the *Rubaiyat*. You know it? Check if you don't."

"I know it, Cap. 'A book of verse beneath a—' "

"You're misquoting, Veem, but that's the one. You'll answer with the last two lines—and get them right. Understood?"

"Yes, Cap. And watch yourself."

The city loomed ahead, buildings stark against the paling sky, the lack of detail giving them almost a two-dimensional effect. A knot of police stood on a corner, one of them calling out as the truck passed.

"Back early, Luchia?"

Kennedy lowered his face over the wheel, waving in a vague manner, pointing to the engine and trying to give the impression that it had caused trouble. The streets were empty aside from men busy with brooms, others collecting garbage. Three blocks from the rendezvous he halted and slipped from the cab. Now was the time of greatest danger.

The hotel was a twin of the first, small, sleazy, a haven for those with no homes but a little cash. Kennedy walked past it, his eyes searching the immediate area and finding nothing suspicious. He had expected it; if the police were waiting they would be in the room, ready to catch Kennedy unawares.

As he passed the door again on the return journey Kennedy slipped inside, one hand on the butt of the needler. The hall was empty, the air heavy with the

scent of dust and rancid oil. By arrangement Luden
would have taken a room under the name of Prin, but
which room? Stepping behind the desk, he found the
register. Luden had taken Room 43, which meant that
in so small a place it must be on the upper floor.

A convenient place in which to set a-trap.

Quietly he climbed the stairs, ears alert for the
slightest sound, catching the murmur of snores, mut-
ters, the creak of sagging springs. Someone whispered
his name.

"Royce!" Kennedy lowered the needler as he saw the
pale face, the strained eyes. "What are you doing
here?"

"Waiting for you. There are two policewomen in
Luden's room."

"How do you know?"

"I heard them arrange it." Royce looked anxiously
past Kennedy up the stairs. "I listened to a message the
police sent to Natalie reporting the capture. That was a
couple of hours ago, while she was at the Council. I got
here in time to see them take Luden to the local pre-
cinct and arrange the trap. I—well, I thought I might
be able to help."

"You can," said Kennedy. "More than you guess.
Now stay well back and don't make a sound."

He continued up the stairs, stepping close to the wall
to avoid creaking treads. Shadows clustered thick at the
head of the stairwell, a pale light struggling through
grimed windows to illuminate closed doors scarred with
flaking paint.

Room 43 lay at the end of a short corridor. Kennedy
stepped softly toward it, listened for a moment, and
then, gripping the knob, turned it and threw open the
panel all in one quick motion.

Two uniformed women were in the room, one lying
on the bed, the other sprawled in a chair. His darts
caught them both before they could make a sound.

"Royce!"

Kennedy dived under the bed as the man entered the
room and closed the door. Dust lay thick under the

sagging springs, obviously undisturbed for weeks. Turning his head, he examined the underside of the mattress. Nothing. Rising, he looked around, seeing a fragment of wood, a pinch of yellow dust caught in a crack. Kneeling, he examined each leg, thick shafts that ended in splayed feet. He lifted the bed, feeling under the leg on the right bottom corner. The crystal fell into his hand.

To Royce he said, "Have you got an aircar?"

"Yes. Natalie lets me use it. It is parked nearby."

"Good." Kennedy heaved the limp figure of the woman from the chair and placed it beside the other on the bed. "Sit down. Relax. Look at what I hold in my hand."

Royce stared at the crystal, bright with little gleams.

"What—"

"Just look at it," urged Kennedy. "See how bright it is, how beautiful. Concentrate on it, that's right, now your eyes are getting a little tired, the lids heavy. There's no reason in the world why you shouldn't close them. Just look at the crystal. Look at it. I'm going to count and when I reach three your eyes are going to close. You want them to close. They are so tired and heavy. One ... two ... three. Good. Now relax. You feel so comfortable, just as if you were floating on a cloud. Nothing bothers you. You feel detached and warm and safe and you can only hear my voice and ..."

His voice droned on, deepening the trance. Kennedy was a master of hypnotism and Royce, dominated all his life, made a perfect subject.

He sighed, becoming limp, relaxing still more as Kennedy massaged certain nerves at the base of his neck. It was an unnecessary precaution, perhaps, for the man had shown his willingness to help, but Kennedy dared take no chances. Hypnotized, conditioned, he would have no choice but to be a willing tool. And, if caught, would know nothing, all posthypnotic commands erased from his memory.

"I shall give you a word. It is 'Veem.' When you

hear it again you will go to your aircar and head to where you found us. You will go farther north to the place where the meteor landed. There is a lake, you will land and wait. Someone will come to you. When he does you will say: 'A book of verses underneath the bough. A jug of wine, a loaf of bread and thou.' He will reply: 'Beside me singing in the wilderness— Oh, wilderness were Paradise enow.' Then, and only then, will you give him what you will find in your pocket."

Kennedy added other instructions designed to protect the man should anything go wrong, then snapped his fingers.

Royce blinked and sat upright.

Kennedy said, "Let's go."

They were only just in time. As he reached the foot of the stairs Kennedy heard the squeal of braking tires, the slam of a car door. Turning, he thrust Royce toward the back of the hotel, to the door opening on the alley. Sharply he said, "Royce, go and find Veem!"

Without looking back Kennedy headed toward the front door, toward the police who came through it, and grabbed him as, unresisting, he raised his arms.

CHAPTER ELEVEN

The officer was disturbed. She said, "This is most irregular, madam. The man is a thief. Charges have been preferred by Henge-Cormile Lan and there are others; evading arrest, assaulting the police, the theft of clothing, an assault against a truck driver, the use of an unpermitted weapon. The sentence will be heavy."

Kennedy would pay, if not with his life then certainly with his brain. Natalie didn't like to think about it. The news of the increased quota had not yet been released.

"I accept full responsibility," she said. "I have already agreed to recompense Henge-Cormile Lan for their loss and they are willing to drop the charges." The arrangement had taken time and a promise of favors to come. "As for the rest, reparation can be made for the clothing."

"And the assaults, madam?"

"They will be answered for. I have said that I will take full responsibitiity for the man while he is in my charge. Of course, if you think that a member of the Council is not to be trusted that is another matter. One which, perhaps, should be taken up with your superior. Major Ella Previn is a friend of mine and I am sure that she will agree the needs of state must be given preference."

The woman, a lieutenant, hesitated. "This is an official matter, then?"

"Why else should I, a member of the Council, have come here in person?" Natalie let impatience edge her voice. "Now hurry! We have wasted too much time as it is. Take me to the prisoner immediately!"

They had not been gentle. Kennedy looked up from where he sat on the edge of the bunk in the narrow cell, bruises on his face, blood on his mouth, more seeping from the reopened gash on his head. Yet despite his injuries, his disheveled appearance, he still radiated dignity, an iron strength.

"My lady." He rose. "It is good of you to take an interest."

"I think you know why."

"The torus?"

"It is where you said it was to be found." She hesitated, then decided to be open. "I will be frank with you. I need your help. If you agree to aid me you can leave here now. If not, both you and the other will pay in a most unpleasant fashion. Do you understand?"

"As raw material for the Zeglar," he said grimly. "As part of your tribute to your masters, the aliens who have enslaved Earth, though you may not be aware of that as yet. Yes, my lady, I understand."

"You are wrong. They guard us. We need them."

"Are you trying to convince yourself or me?" Kennedy shrugged at her expression. "I think that you may have learned a little since we last met. If not, you are less intelligent than I think. Luden?"

"He is at my house under guard. You can join him if you agree to help me."

"How?"

"You said that you came in a ship," she said quickly. "Can you prove that? Please, it is important."

Unconsciously she had betrayed herself, such a woman reared in such a culture would demand, never plead. And yet she had just done that, and to a man.

"I can prove it," said Kennedy. "But first I want something. My chronometer. The police took it together with the gun and some money I had. The gun they can keep, the money also, but I need the watch."

"You shall have it."

"And something else. You want me to help you, and I will do it, but in return you must help me. Agreed?"

For a moment she hesitated, hating to be obligated to a man, but promises made could always be broken.

"Agreed. Now let us leave this place."

Luden was busy when Kennedy arrived. He sat at a table in the library, the board littered with books, papers, sheaves of calculations. He looked tired, his face sunken with fatigue, sleepless hours of strain during which he had worked with a grim persistence.

"Cap!" He rose and stepped forward. "You're hurt!"

"Only a little, Jarl." Kennedy had washed, wearing clean denims, a patch of adhesive over the wound on his scalp. "Have you learned anything?"

"A little. The crystal?"

"I found it. Royce was taking it to the *Mordain* under hypnotic instruction. We'll know if it got there when Natalie gives me my communicator."

Kennedy looked around the library. The shelves were well-stocked, old volumes mixed with new, rolls of maps resting in a cabinet. The door was of thick wood, locked, watchful guards positioned outside. The windows were barred, set high above the ground, the panes small and ringed with iron. The gaping maw of a fireplace narrowed to a chimney too small to enter.

Natalie was taking no chances.

"An unusual woman," said Luden when Kennedy had completed his examination. "And a sick one. She is suffering from hypertension probably caused by the malfunction of certain ductless glands and aggravated by a heart condition. With rest and care she could live to a ripe old age, but she seems determined to burn herself out while still comparatively young."

"A power complex?"

"Yes, Cap, and it could kill her. I tried to warn her, but she was most curt."

Kennedy smiled, guessing the woman's reaction to the well-meant advice. She would not have taken it from a woman, much less a man.

"However, she has been informative in her way. She has managed to get herself into an invidious position with her colleagues on the Council and is fighting to save her career. We can restore her to power if we can prove we landed in a vessel that passed through the defensive ring. From what I can gather she is locked in intense rivalry with a Teri Kramer, who is the chief of Aerial Command."

"And a tool of the Zeglar?"

"Very probably, Cap, and a willing one. There is no other way to account for the lie they substantiated." Luden added dryly, "I managed to obtain her cooperation to a certain degree. Enough at least to allow me to make a limited investigation."

He indicated the books, maps, and photographs among the papers. The photographs were crude compared to those the men had known, but details were clear enough.

"Taken from the Luna observatory, Cap. She ordered them to be taken at dawn and they were transmitted by radio."

The torus, positive proof that they had not lied. Kennedy dropped them, and picked up some of the books.

"The library here contains works not available to the general public," said Luden. "Military and technical manuals together with scientific reports, many of them made at the time of first contact with the Zeglar. Earth is surrounded by those triple-coned forts we saw. They are in permanent orbits and carry human personnel. They also carry a cyborg computer, and it is my guess they are in direct contact with the Zeglar in their headquarters at the North Pole."

"Here on Earth, Jarl?"

"Yes, Cap. It surprised me as it does you. They have built a fortress in the ice from which they control their space fleet by, I assume, a system of relays connected to space stations. What they term raw material is delivered to them at the pole for processing. The bomb that tore our hull was one of thousands drifting in orbit to form an aerial mine field. The only safe passage through the atmosphere is by two channels, one at either hemisphere and both over the ocean at the equator."

And there were other ships in space, sleek interceptors, massive forts, garrisons of the Zeglar.

Earth enclosed, entrapped, sealed against any escape or interference.

"We should have Commander Olsen here," Kennedy said grimly. "MALACA 1 would soon take care of the Zeglar."

"True, Cap," said Luden. "But we cannot summon aid until we return back through the torus, and even then we'll still be faced with the problem of closing it." He riffled some of his papers. "Some things I have learned. The early reports are mostly concerned with the Zeglarian weaponry. I assume they must have given a series of demonstrations in order to convince those then in power of the wisdom of cooperation. We can discount all but one: the green force that distorts the gravitons. I am inclined to believe it is a form of subspatial warp that attacks matter on an extra-dimensional plane. The torus, as far as we can tell, also exists on a plane other than the normal continuum. It cannot be in a state of perfect equilibrium, otherwise the orange ring would not be seen. Therefore, if the energy of the alien projectors could be directed in sufficient concentration against the torus, it is possible it could upset the present balance."

"Which could result in two things," reminded Kennedy. "Either the torus closes or expands. It's a gamble, Jarl."

"Yes, Cap, but it is a risk we must take. I cannot see any other possibility of ending the threat to Earth."

Kennedy stood for a moment before the table, thinking, then he walked to the door and beat on it with his fist.

"Be quiet in there!" The voice was from one of the guards, deep, strong, almost masculine. "Be silent!"

Kennedy continued beating at the panel. As it jerked open to reveal an angry face, he snapped, "Get Natalie Toluca at once!"

"How dare you!"

"Do it!" The crack of his voice was like the lash of a whip. "It is a matter of urgency that affects her life! Run, damn you, before we burn down the house!"

She came, fuming with rage, barely able to control her anger.

"What do you want? How dare you disturb me. I was arranging a meeting of the Council, summoning them here so as to listen to your evidence. Must I remind you of what you are? Prisoners in my charge? Would you rather be back in jail?"

"Please do not upset yourself," urged Luden. "Such violent emotion can only aggravate your condition and—"

"Shut your mouth!"

"And shut yours!" snapped Kennedy. Reaching behind her, he slammed the door in the face of the startled guard. "If you want to save your neck you'll listen and do as I say. Have you ever had personal contact with the Zeglar?"

"What?" The question surprised her, threw her off balance. "No. Not in the flesh."

"But you've seen them on a screen? Good. Describe what they look like."

Luden frowned as she ended. "There are similarities to the Nemarch, Cap; but would they have traveled so far?"

"In a different universe there could have been a different evolution, Jarl. We know the Nemarch only as nest-dwellers, but here they could have discovered spaceflight. And their choice of the Pole is significant."

"Even so, Cap, there are variations. They could be a branch that died out in our own continuum to survive in this. If so—"

"What are you talking about?" Natalie glanced from one to the other. "And why are you curious about the Zeglar?"

"Before you can defeat an enemy you have to know it," said Kennedy. "And the Zeglar is an enemy, have no doubt as to that."

"You can't be sure."

"I'm positive. The facts speak for themselves." Kennedy gestured at the table, the litter of books and papers. "What you call the Zeglar we know as the Nemarch. Cold-blooded, vicious, hampered only by their lack of technical skill. Their planet is a cold one, and to them, humanity is a source of food. That is what you are, you and everyone else on this planet. Food and raw material for their machines. When you stop giving it to them freely they will take as much as they want. Damn it, woman, can't you see what's happened? Are you so involved in your petty squabbles that you can't imagine a greater threat? What does a seat on the Council matter against an enslaved world?"

The raw violence in his voice dissolved the last of her anger. Once again she felt the disturbance of his nearness, the domination of his will.

Watching her, Luden knew that Kennedy's words had stirred buried doubts, triggered subconscious anxieties which rose to flower into ugly bloom.

Shaken, she said, "What can I do?"

"First, my chronometer. Thank you." Kennedy threw it toward Luden, who caught it in one thin hand. "Have you a warehouse or factory close to the city that can be cleared and ready for immediate use? Somewhere a vessel could be hidden? Good. Jarl?"

Luden lifted his head from the communicator.

"Success, Cap. Royce delivered the crystal and the *Mordain* is fully operational."

"Royce?" Natalie's voice echoed her incredulity. "My consort?"

"A good man," said Kennedy. "With more courage than you'd guess. And he loves you. God alone knows why, but he does. You should be glad to have him."

Memory flushed her cheeks. "You wouldn't say that if you knew. He's natural-born."

"So what? Isn't he still a man?"

"Yes, I suppose so, but——" She broke off, putting

aside the concept for later consideration. "What happens now?"

"That's simple," said Kennedy. "We are going to make you the Supreme Head of the Council of the Nord-Am Quadrant."

CHAPTER **TWELVE**

The ease of it had amazed her. Even now when the thing had been done and she lay in her bed watching the pale light of dawn at the windows, she still couldn't believe what had actually happened. And yet it had only been what she'd expected, Teri Kramer deposed and now held incommunicado, Helen Estaler accepting her defeat with good grace, Tana Golchika swallowing her pride, the others, all of them, eager to fawn.

And Kennedy had stage-managed it all.

Stretching, feeling oddly at peace, she saw it all for the dozenth time. The upper chamber, the Council assembled, waiting, the atmosphere heavy with impatience. There had been barely veiled sneers, innuendos far from subtle, the first bubbles of the rising froth of scandal which they were certain would engulf her.

And then Kennedy, demanding, Luden explaining, his thin voice like a slashing knife as he cut down all doubt, all protestation. And then the moment when Kennedy had lifted his arm and had spoken two words.

"Now, Penza!"

A moment and then the ship had appeared. The vessel which the Zeglar had sworn did not exist. And the actual proof had overwhelmed them all.

And Kennedy again, demanding, threatening a little, beating down all opposition with the sheer force of his personality.

Now she was the undisputed head of the Council and could rest at last.

The illusion was quickly shattered.

A knock and Royce entered the chamber, a cup of tisane in one hand, a list in the other. As she sipped the

108

warm brew, he said, "Natalie, Cap wants you to do something. He said it was very important."

Cap? She felt a little resentful of the familiarity that had sprung up between Royce and the strangers.

"What does he want?"

"Your signed authority to order equipment on immediate priority. Teri Kramer to be released and placed in his charge. Communication to be made with the Zeglar at noon. There are some other things—"

"Give me that!" Snatching the paper, she ran her eyes over the list. "When did you get this?"

"Veem just delivered it. He wanted to see you, but you were resting and, well, I thought it best to bring it to you myself."

Together with the tisane, which undoubtedly held soothing medications, she thought. Was it consideration or calculated manipulation? It would be Royce who was responsible. Kennedy, burdened with other matters, would have had no time to pander to the weakness of a prideful woman. But why had Kennedy asked for Teri Kramer?

She rose, suddenly suspicious, ignoring the robe Royce held out to her. She had slept too long, and who knew what conspiracies had been hatched in the recent hours?

As she dressed, she said, "I'll sign the authorization for equipment and you will deliver it. The rest I will handle myself, if I think it wise."

"Please, Natalie. Cap knows what he is doing."

"True, but for whose benefit? Do as I say, Royce." She saw his hurt expression as if he had been a dog who, anticipating a pat, had received a kick instead. More gently she said, "Don't be overwhelmed by their friendship. Remember that their concern is for their own world, not ours."

"A bargain was made, Natalie."

"It will be kept. Each to help the other. They have kept their part and I will keep mine. But I want to know what is going on. I have no intention of allowing them to leave this world in a shambles."

During the morning she worked to consolidate her position, making agreements with heads of other Quadrants, delaying, negotiating, weaving a web of power and political advantage. As the sun neared the zenith she collected the erstwhile chief of Aerial Command and took her to the great warehouse that held the *Mordain*.

The place was a hive of activity, women sweating as they supervised toiling men, a mass of equipment set against one wall, screens and monitoring devices of a dozen kinds staffed by technicians whose eyes were bright at new discoveries.

The ship itself was covered with workers, masked women welding a complex lattice of copper bands over the hull, their work checked and tested by a giant who roared commands.

"You're slacking! Check and double-check each junction. I want the ratio to be absolute. Damn it, don't you know how to weld a joint?"

A tough amazon lifted her mask and said, scowling, "You big ape! Open that great mouth of yours just once more and I'll ram this torch down your throat."

Saratov grinned. "You and what army? Now get busy, girl, or I'll come up there and paddle your rear."

Amazingly, she accepted the insult, perhaps because she knew he could do exactly as he threatened.

At Natalie's side Teri Kramer said, "Why am I here? What is going on?"

Only Kennedy could answer those questions. He turned as they approached, setting aside the tool with which he had been working. He had, Natalie realized, been working through the night as had the others, but his face showed no trace of fatigue.

"You've brought the woman, good." He looked at Teri. "I want the truth. Have you ever made private contact with the Zeglar?"

"If you mean have I spoken to them without others present the answer is that I have. But it was my right—"

"Never mind that," interrupted Kennedy. "I'm not

accusing you of anything. What I'm doing is giving you a chance to redeem yourself. To get back your rank and position. Right, Natalie?"

Suspicious, she said, "I'm not sure about that. Just what is it you want?"

"Her willing cooperation. If she gives it, will you make a deal?"

Natalie had no choice but to agree—and promises could always be broken.

"Good." Kennedy turned to the other woman, who stood, puzzled, among her guards. "Now, Teri, this is what I want you to do." His instructions were explicit, and to Natalie, utterly without sense. He ended, "Don't invent information, but make certain they understand. How soon, Jarl?"

Lifting his head from a mass of equipment, Luden said, "A few minutes, Cap. Veem is in position and we are almost ready. You'd better take the woman into the booth."

It was small, set up in a corner of the warehouse, a screen set on a stand in the middle. Kennedy stood Teri before it, stepped behind it to where he could watch a monitor and a panel of dials. Natalie joined him, refusing to be excluded.

"Make no sound or gesture," he warned. "This is more important than you guess. Ready, Teri?"

"Yes."

"Just one other thing," Kennedy said quietly. "As a woman your loyalty should be with your own kind, but if it is not, if you should betray us, then you will never leave this booth alive."

Looking at his face, the woman knew he meant it.

"Please! Don't look at me like that! I'll cooperate!"

The screen flashed into life.

Looking at the monitor, Kennedy thinned his lips as he studied the visage. The similarities to the Nemarch were plain, but, as Luden had guessed, the Zeglar were of a divergent branch.

"What do you want?" The alien stared at the

woman, the obvious signs of her distress. "Is something wrong?"

"Everything! That ship that penetrated the defenses—you know?"

"There was no ship."

"There was and we both know it. I'm not talking from the Council now; I'm trying to warn you. It was a ship and it's hidden in the lake close to where we thought it crashed. It didn't crash. The effects were created by an atomic torpedo."

"Atomic?"

"Yes, I can't explain, but that's what it was. Maybe you can check." Teri was not acting, the raw anxiety in her voice was real, her face reflected terror. "Those in the ship said it had come through the torus and that others would follow, but that isn't the worst of it. They are going to destroy your base at the North Pole!"

"They cannot! It is not possible!"

"I'm only telling you what they said. Warning you. If you don't want to be destroyed they have to be stopped."

"How do you know this?"

"They contacted us. I received the message and as yet I've managed to keep it secret. They came through the torus and destroyed one of your forts. I—" Teri broke off, simulating fear. "Someone's coming. I have to go. But act fast while you've the chance!"

The screen died as Kennedy cut the connection. As it faded he said, "Teri, my congratulations. You did a wonderful job. Natalie, she should be rewarded, and I am sure that you are a woman who keeps her word."

"We can both keep it," said Teri. "Natalie, about Royce, I promise that I won't breathe a word of—well, you know."

Pacts, promises, the manipulations of political diplomacy, abruptly Natalie was tired of it. She looked at the panel of instruments, wishing she understood what it was all about.

"Why did you have Teri tell the Zeglar what she

did? If you intend to destroy their base, why warn them?"

"We need allies," said Kennedy. "This way we hope to get them."

"Allies?"

"The brains the aliens have enslaved." Kennedy led the way from the booth and gestured toward the assembled equipment, the technicians concentrating on their instruments. "Earth brains, Natalie, an integral part of the cyborg computers that control the ships and forts of the Zeglar. Can you realize what it must be to exist in such a condition? No," he continued without waiting for an answer. "You can't. If you did, you would never have agreed to supply the raw material. Those brains are alive and aware of what has happened to them. Do you think they have any love for the creatures who own them?"

"We didn't know," said Teri. "We thought that only the basic cells were used. That the ego would not survive."

"You're lying!" Kennedy was harsh. "You knew. You're too intelligent not to know. Well, the thing is done, now we hope to use it."

"There will be no more," said Natalie. "At least not from the Nord-Am Quadrant. If I accomplish nothing else at least I will do that."

Teri said quietly, "How do you hope to use the brains?"

"A cyborg unit is never allowed to be independent," said Kennedy. "Remember the brain is alive and with a will of its own. There had to be a means of enforcing obedience and it is done by inserting thin wires into the pleasure and pain centers of the brain. A minute current passed through the wires activates the selected node and will produce either pleasure or pain. A pleasure so intense that it is literal ecstasy, agony so concentrated that it is a virtual hell. The pulses are controlled by radio. Orders to the cyborgs must also be transmitted by radio—there can be no other way for the

Zeglar to direct their vessels. We are trying to isolate the frequency used."

"And then?"

"We'll turn the cyborgs against their masters."

Luden came running towards the little group. "Cap! We are picking up something. Veem reports the movement of a fort from its normal path."

"Toward where we landed, Jarl?"

"Yes. They must be checking the area for residual radioactivity. Finding it will be proof of what they have been told. When they do they will undoubtedly destroy the lake and all it contains." Luden frowned. "I wish we didn't have to rely on these crude instruments, Cap. It is important that we gain full knowledge of the forces they employ."

"We'll get it, Jarl." Kennedy led the way toward a bank of screens. "Let's watch the action."

For long minutes nothing happened, and Natalie brooded on the implications of what she saw. The scanners must have been placed the previous night, set on trees and rocks under cover of darkness. The equipment and the technicians who attended it must have been arranged while she slept. The plan must have been in Kennedy's mind from the beginning.

She heard Teri draw in her breath.

The screens showed the lake from various directions, the hill, scarred and torn, against which the supposed meteor had landed. As she watched something fell toward it, the first of a hail which rained from the skies, dark objects that expanded into flame as they hit. The satellite bombs of the aerial mine field.

"Why bombs?" whispered Luden, then, "Of course, they are clearing a path for the fort."

In the screens the hill, the lake, and the surrounding shores were torn and pulverized by the incessant rain of explosives. Half of the scanners were knocked out, and the scene was now revealed in restricted directions. Dazed, imagining the pulsing roar that must fill the area, Natalie watched, knowing now why the pictures were unaccompanied by sound.

Teri said softly, "Look at it. Nothing could live under such a bombardment."

The Zeglar knew better. Water made a good shield and a strong defense against such primitive weapons. If the ship they assumed to be under the water was efficient, then, as yet, it would be relatively unharmed.

As the rain of missiles ceased, Luden said sharply, "Get ready. Full instrumentation as ordered."

A shadow fell over the scene, a triple-pointed patch of darkness, the center of it steadying over the lake as if a distant marksman were taking careful aim.

"Filters, Jarl. Girls, close your eyes!"

Light blazed from the darkened screens as Kennedy gave the order. A searing, writhing turmoil of emerald flame. From a long moment it hung as if a thing alive, roiling, pulsing, and then it vanished.

And with it went the entire lake.

Natalie stared unbelievingly at the totally altered scene. The hill was gone. The water. The edging vegetation. Where once had lain a lake blue and calm beneath the sun was now only a gaping hole, the sides seared as if by intense heat.

The fury of the Zeglar.

How could any man, even with friends, with only a single vessel, hope to defeat it?

CHAPTER THIRTEEN

The sound was a susurration of clicks, intermittent, forming no recognizable pattern. Standing tense in the laboratory of the *Mordain* Royce listened, looking at the two men who sat at the table. Kennedy and Luden were engrossed in calculations, playing and replaying the record until the clicks seemed to have become a part of Royce's body, echoed in the beating of his heart.

"Here." Chemile thrust a cup of coffee into Royce's hand. "Try it. It's good, isn't it?"

Royce sipped and nodded. "Very good."

"I wish Penza had heard that! Cap! Jarl! You hear the man? He likes my coffee."

"He probably thinks you'd throw him out if he said different," boomed a voice from the open port. Saratov, grimy but smiling, held out his hand for coffee. Tasting it, he pursed his lips as if to spit. "As I thought. Royce is being polite."

"Shut up, Penza!" snapped Chemile. "What are you doing in here, anyway? You're supposed to be working on the shield."

"It's done." Saratov drank more of the coffee. "Those women can work if they've a mind to. All I have to do now is to run leads to the generator. You'll have to check the oscillation of the harmonics, Jarl. One step out and away goes our defenses."

Royce said, "Will it work?"

"Theoretically, yes," said Luden. He leaned back in his chair, one thin hand holding his cup of coffee, his voice adopting the familiar tone of a lecturer. "Basically it is possible to cancel out one force by means of

116

another. For example, if you should fire a bullet at someone, and he fired back at the same time and in exactly the right direction, the two missiles would collide and each negate the force of the other. The energy would not be lost, of course, but would be transmuted to heat. As far as I can determine the Zeglar use a force which operates on a vibratory principle. You could use light or sound as an analogy. Now, if we can generate a complimentary force in the copper bands, one of exactly the right frequency, we should be able to heterodyne most of its destructive elements. Unfortunately the information delivered by the screens was distorted by the medium that transmitted it. And there are other complications I will not go into now. The hope is that we shall be able to withstand Zeglar fire for at least a short period and diminish its effects for a longer one."

"And if the shield doesn't work?"

Luden shrugged. "In that case we shall be in a most unfortunate position."

Kennedy said, "Shouldn't you be with Natalie, Royce?"

"She said I could stay, but if you want me to leave—"

"No, Royce, you can stay, but let me make one thing clear. You can't go with us."

Deep inside of him Royce felt a thread of hope wither and die. A vague and foolish hope, perhaps, but one born of his liking for the men, the different way of life they enjoyed. Looking at him, Kennedy sensed the disappointment.

"You can't go with us," he said again. "Not because we don't like you, but in our universe you would have no place. Here you have. Natalie needs you, but it is more than that. It's time something was done to correct the imbalance of the sexes. Neither men nor women should be dominant. They are partners, each with areas in which they specialize, but always able to work as equals. You could help to bring that about. It will be slow and hard, but it can be done. It has to be done if this world is going to survive.

"The galaxy is full of other races. One day, maybe, they will contact you or you will contact them. When that day comes men and women must have learned to work together. If they haven't, then once again Earth will be enslaved."

Bitterly Royce said, "You should tell that to Natalie."

"I will, but I think she knows it already. You know, Royce, on our world we have a saying. The power behind the throne. You could be that power."

"With what?"

"The knowledge we will give you. New technologies, information you have lost, ways to build, to obtain atomic power, to build weapons and spaceships. It won't come at once, Royce, but in a few generations Earth will be ready to expand, and when it is men will be the equals of women."

Leaning forward, Kennedy touched a control and once again the susurration of clicks filled the air. Royce frowned.

"What is that?"

"The code used by the Zeglar to direct their vessels. We managed to isolate it. Now we have to decode it. Once we do, every vessel of the aliens will be ours to command."

"Maybe not, Cap," Luden said precisely. "Those forts ringing Earth, yes; but they could have another code for the ones in space. However, you are correct in one thing. Now that we know their frequency we can at least blanket their communications. Now about this code." He paused, frowning. "It must contain a pleasure-pain impulse, which would of necessity be repeated. Pain for delay, pleasure for instant obedience. That is logical. Unfortunately we have very little on which to work."

"More than enough, Jarl. For one thing the code has to be translatable into a language the brains understand. That gives us an advantage. Directional points, velocities, position, orders to fire and cease firing—it's just a matter of time."

The record was speeded, slowed, run through the computer a thousand times in a search for familiar associations. The Zeglar helped them. As day turned into night a message came from Chemile, who was stationed at a local observatory.

"Cap! Some of the forts are moving. They seem to be forming a new pattern over the North Pole."

Quickly Luden adjusted his instruments. From the speakers came more of the clicks.

"Veem, report on all movements. Check for minor diversions and positional changes. One instruction, observed, could give us the key."

"They could be using scramble, Jarl," said Saratov from the door of the laboratory. Royce had gone, laden with microfilm. The warehouse was empty of workers, the electronic apparatus dismantled now that the need for it was over.

"They probably are, Penza," agreed Luden. "Not that it matters. We are only interested in isolating each message-impulse. In any case scramble would hardly be necessary in instructing the brains."

"How's that?"

"No words," said Kennedy. He listened for a moment to the drone of Chemile's voice, Luden correlating the messages with the series of clicks. "You don't have to talk to a horse if you want it to move, just touch it with a whip or spur. The same to guide it, the pressure of the reins is enough. The only time the Zeglar would need to communicate in words is when they talk directly to the crew."

"Women," said the giant uneasily. "Cap, if you manage to override the Zeglar control and crash those vessels, the women—"

"They will have a chance to escape, Penza. The forts are equipped with emergency pods. They can bail out and parachute down."

Luden grunted as Chemile ceased talking. "Cap, I think we have it. Listen." He touched controls and ran a thin finger over a sheet of paper. "That was when one of the forts moved to the left. And now this." Again the clicks. "One rose to form the tip of a defensive cone. Two incidents and each is followed by this." From the recorder came a triple blur of clicks. "I would say that it represents the pleasure-impulse. A reward for obedience."

"They're frightened," said Kennedy. "They can't be certain they destroyed the ship they were told was in the lake. Or they believe there is another. In any case they are moving the forts to protect their base at the Pole. Convenient."

"And dangerous," said Luden. "If they are on the defensive every fort will be on the alert. Once we move they will spot us."

"And we're not in the best of condition," the giant said grimly. "I did my best to tune the coils but could only get them to five places, the bare minimum. And I'm not too happy about the compensator. That crystal isn't pure zirnalite. It's close and will do the job, but if too much strain is put on it, it could blow."

"At times, Penza," Luden said acidly, "your pessimism amazes me. Tell me, is there anything we could do to improve the *Mordain?*"

"With what we have, no."

"Then whatever the condition we must accept it. Right, Cap?"

"Right," said Kennedy. "It's not like you to be so down. Why don't you go and collect Veem while Jarl and I figure out this code?"

Once the key had been found it was simple. Kennedy listened to the series of clicks, made fresh recordings, and assembled a panel as Luden checked the shield-generator. When the professor returned he explained what he had done.

"I've rigged variable repeaters, Jarl. Loops to carry the code with a means to cover a wide band. You'll have to select the right frequency as well as operate the panel. See? This button for pleasure, this for pain, the rest to cover various directional instructions."

"As well as one to give the order to fire?"

"Of course. The red one there."

"I must familiarize myself with the assembly, Cap. And then, I take it, we shall be ready to leave?"

"Yes, Jarl. Suits and battle stations. We'll go when the others return."

They left an hour after midnight, when the city was sleeping and the stars shone clear. From a high window Royce watched them go, seeing the slender shape of the *Mordain* occlude the stars and vanish in the night. He heard the rustle of garments and sensed rather than saw the woman at his side.

"They've gone, Royce?"

"Yes, Natalie, they've gone."

"And you wanted to go with them." Her hand touched his arm, pressed with unspoken sympathy. "I know. Kennedy told me and told me why he couldn't take you. I think he was right."

He made no reply and she sensed his disappointment, something of his loss, a loss she shared. Never to see Kennedy again. Never to feel the strange disturbance he had created within her being. The stranger had changed her life, and she would never see him again. No matter what happened in space she was sure of that. He would succeed or die trying.

"Royce!"

"You should be resting, Natalie. Asleep."

Again she touched him, remembering, knowing that never again could she consider him as a fashionable appendage. Kennedy had taught her that. The conditioning of a lifetime would die hard, but it would die, she would see to that.

"I can't sleep, Royce, and neither can you. Not yet, not until we know."

Would Earth be free or would the Zeglar survive to tighten their grip? One man would decide it. Decide the fate of a world.

Royce said, as if he had read her thoughts, "They must be near the Pole by now."

CHAPTER **FOURTEEN**

A sheet of ice and snow lay white beneath the summer sun. The endless expanse was unmarked by anything recognizable, a few huts, a rift, cracked ice, nothing that pinpointed the Zegler base.

Kennedy narrowed his eyes at the screen, judging time and distance, knowing that a mistake would cost their lives. Too high, and he risked the satellite bombs; too low, a blast of fire from a hidden projector could sear them without warning. Yet, how else to find the base?

"Penza, keep full power going into the shield. Jarl, can you locate the origin of the broadcasts?"

"I think so, Cap. A point ahead to the right."

The directions could mean nothing, the transmitter could be miles from the base, but it was a guide if nothing else. And the aliens, lulled by a century of security, could have grown careless.

"Ready the torps, Veem. One should do it. All we want to do is to draw their fire."

"Let's hope they don't aim straight, Cap," Chemile said grimly. "Torp ready as ordered."

"Jarl?"

"Reception strong, Cap. Fading, now!"

Chemile fired the torpedo, watching from the turret as it flashed to the ice, filters protecting his eyes from the savage glare as it burst in sun-bright fury. Steam rose, plumes of vapor, shattered fragments of the ice cap, and from a point two miles to the left, a shaft of emerald flame.

"Cap!"

Kennedy had anticipated Chemile's warning; already

122

the *Mordain* was lifting, turning to run from the threat.

"Jarl!"

Luden thrust his hands at the panel, the hastily in-stalled aparatus, blanketing the local broadcast, using the full power of the *Mordain*'s generators to drive his signal to the forts above.

Down! Down! Down!

Each instruction preceded by a blast of pain, fol-lowed by a jolt of pleasure.

High above explosions shook the air, the satellite bombs blasting against the hulls of the descending forts. Again Luden stabbed at the buttons. A long burst of pleasure and then, *"Fire! Fire! Fire!"*

Green flame washed the heavens, reached the bombs, detonated them, passed on toward the ice below. Like a scalded cat the *Mordain* darted away from the lambent fury, almost caught in the blast.

From the turret Chemile yelled, "Jarl! You're on our side, remember?"

"Stand ready for defensive fire, Veem," snapped Kennedy. "We're going up."

Air whined past the hull, a thin sound which rose to a shriek before dying as they reached the upper atmo-sphere. A fort loomed before them, dropped below, an-other, two more, and Luden jammed the orders from the base below to destroy the vessel that rose so close. Again he pressed his buttons, and like monstrous snow-flakes, the forts began to fall.

They tilted, spinning a little, veering from side to side, accelerating as pods jetted from them, the crews abandoning the vessels which no longer responded to their commands.

The base opened fire. Green flame rose from a score of giant projectors, burning the very air, dimming the sun with their fury, reaching up toward the menacing shapes that fell from the skies. Power enough, perhaps, to negate the threat, to burn and dissolve the forts and dissipate their mass over the ice cap.

Kennedy turned the *Mordain*.

"Veem! Jarl!"

Three atomic torpedoes slammed into the center of the defensive ring of flame, gouging a vast crater, revealing thick metal, torn compartments, massed machines. More fire came from the falling vessels, emerald fury to match that of the crippled base, to overwhelm it, to fill the burning air with a fog of gusting steam, vapor, boiling water, tremendous boulders of ice.

And the forts followed the fire, massed tons of dead weight, their cyborg computers lost in an ecstasy of pleasure, crashing one after the other to destroy the base and all it contained.

From space, they watched it clear on the screens, the awful devastation that seared the cancer of alien invasion from this twin of Earth.

"We did it, Cap!" Chemile was triumphant. "We wiped them out and didn't even get scratched!'

"Good work, Jarl." Kennedy searched the screens. "But it isn't over yet. There have to be other vessels, interceptors at least. I didn't see any follow the forts."

"I would assume they are assembled at the torus, Cap. The Zeglar must have guessed we came through it, the fort we destroyed would have reported the attack, and they are probably taking precautions."

MALACA 1 had done the same on the other side. Defensive might had been assembled and positioned to destroy any offensive vessel coming through the ring.

"Too many ships, Jarl." Kennedy touched a control. The screens had been adapted; if the vessels were using an ocular invisibility they would be revealed. Still nothing.

"Tycho," boomed Saratov. "They could be based there, Cap. It makes sense."

"As far as we know the Zeglar were all on Earth," said Luden. "The Nemarch hate low gravity and it is logical to assume that the Zeglar do also. And there would have been no point in their having a base on the moon. A ship depot, perhaps, but if so it would be a supply point for vessels only, with maybe a few humans to attend to the loading facilities."

They dared not leave the force intact if Earth was to

be wholly cleansed of the invader. Kennedy fed power
to the engines and frowned at the sluggish response.
Long accustomed to highly tuned coils it was disturbing to Kennedy to find the *Mordain* had lost its normal efficiency.

Even so, within minutes the moon loomed huge in
the screens, the great rayed crater of Tycho, the ships
rising like a swarm of disturbed hornets.

"Jarl!"

"Trouble, Cap. They are not responding. I can
discover no sign of transmitted signals; they must be
operating as independent units on a set program. Their
cyborgs probably contain Zeglarian brains. As interceptors their task is to hunt down and destroy any vessel
that does not match recognizable patterns."

Kennedy watched them as they came, long, sleek, tapering sterns ringed with coils of lambent green fire, the
destructive force of the projectors adapted for propul-
sion.

"Veem!"

The range was too great for effective use of the
Dione, the ships too widely scattered to make full use
of the torpedoes, but the sprom cannon could spew
space with destruction. Chemile hit the release, sending
a stream of self-propelled missiles into the path of the
interceptors. As three of the slender shapes exploded
into ruin he clamped his hands on the controls and sent
the *Mordain* hurtling toward the torus.

The alien ships followed, closing, threads of emerald
flame reaching out before them.

The *Mordain* shuddered as they hit.

The ship dodged, and Kennedy felt its slight drag.
The stars blurred to steady as he engaged hydrive. The
interceptors fell away to suddenly reappear even closer
than before.

Again the *Mordain* shuddered.

Chemile fired back from the turret, the blast of the
Dione meeting a green lance, negating it, opposed
forces blossoming in eye-bright splendor. The sprom
cannon pulsed, spouting missiles, the leading interceptor

dissolving in brilliant energy. Another, and then the *Mordain* jerked, the hull vibrating as if screaming in agony.

"Penza!"

"The shield, Cap, it's not holding." The giant's voice held pain. "And the compensator's going. Cap! You've got to dodge that energy!"

A thing easier said than done, but Kennedy did his best. The drag was getting worse as the compensator lost efficiency, the crushing weight of gravitational drag more apparent at each maneuver. Sweating, blood oozing from nose and ears, the controls dimming beyond his faceplate, he fought to save the *Mordain* and their lives.

To dodge at such velocities was to invite instant death. To maintain a straight and relatively safe path was to offer a perfect target to the alien vessels already dangerously close. Their only hope lay in speed.

"Penza, the coils!"

"I'm trying, Cap." Saratov had thrown back his helmet and stood crouched against the engine, one ear to the humped mass, his fingers resting on a row of adjustment verniers. Sweat beaded his shaved skull, and ran into his eyes narrowed with concentration. He ignored it as he concentrated on the delicate balance of the coils within. Three of them were set at right angles to each other. The coils had to be at a high peak of similarity for the hydrive to work at all. And now they had to be tuned to an even finer pitch if Saratov hoped to increase the velocity.

Normal ship engineers used delicate monitors and could take hours to tune an engine. Saratov used only his bare hands, natural senses, and trained skill to do it within minutes.

"Keep firing, Veem," said Kennedy. "We've got to give Penza a chance. Still no luck, Jarl?"

"I am doing my best, Cap." Luden's voice betrayed the strain he was under. "As yet without success."

"Concentrate on the pleasure-impulse, Jarl. If they are Zeglarian brains I doubt if the pain center would have been involved." He breathed his relief as the interceptors fell back. "Penza's managed to tune the coils. Now for the torus."

He could see it ahead, a thick cluster of vessels around the orange ring, green fire playing on it from all sides.

Chemile's voice rang from the helmet radio. "Cap! They're closing it! We're trapped!"

The torus was smaller now but still large enough to permit the *Mordain* to pass through if they could get there in time. A greater hazard was the ships ringing it, the monstrous fort that held the remainder of the Zeglar.

"Cap! I think I have found the correct signal. At least the ships are no longer firing."

"Pleasure, Jarl?"

"Yes, Cap. I am maintaining a continuous transmission, as you can hear."

Kennedy listened to the sequence of clicks, his eyes narrowed as he looked at the torus ahead, the circle of ships, the great fort. The vessels were capable of filling space with energies the *Mordain* could not withstand. Yet the torus could only be reached by running the gauntlet of fire.

Kennedy slowed the ship, the interceptors coming up from behind, passing, their projectors dead, their cyborg computers lost in a continuous ecstasy.

He could use those missiles. He could follow their curtain of protection.

He had aimed directly for the torus, the interceptors had followed him and were continuing ahead on the same path. The ships around and before the ring ignored them, programmed to recognize them as allies.

The fort realized the danger too late.

Green fire blazed, slender shapes dissolving, more escaping the destruction to pass on, hitting the cluster of vessels as if they were pellets fired from a shotgun. Space flamed with released energies, emerald fire dulling the stars, the orange ring.

"Fire torps, Veem!"

The desperate chance had to be taken. The fort was barely damaged; it had dealt, not received, destruction. A glancing blow from one of the interceptors sent it toward the torus.

It fired as the *Mordain* neared, the copper bands of the improvised shield glowing, fuming to vapor, exposing the hull to the full fury of the blast.

Chemile fired back.

A rain of torpedoes gouged into the massive hull, exploding, adding the blue-white glare of destroyed atoms to the green fury of the alien projectors.

The blast was too near, too close.

Kennedy felt the *Mordain* jerk, air gusting from the ripped hull, the controls sluggish, the crushing weight of gravitational forces dulling his vision as, desperately, he fought to return the vessel to its original path.

The orange ring was close, dangerously so, a fraction of misjudgment and they would hit it.

"Cap! The fort! It's coming after us!"

"Blast it, Veem!"

Kennedy bit his lips, concentrating, narrowing his vision to the torus, the destructive ring, the curtain of black that he must hit before the fort could complete the destruction of the *Mordain.*

And then they were through, lancing between the clustered ships of MALACA 1, slowing as Chemile fired the last of the torpedoes at the fort which had tried to follow them. The missiles hit, exploded, and filled the area with released energies, a sunbright glare of emerald that twisted space and destroyed the balance of forces which permitted the torus to exist.

Then there was nothing but a fading orange ring that closed and puckered and vanished as if it had never been.